THE
BLACKTHORN
CHRONICLES

This book is a work of fiction. Names, characters, organizations, places, events, and incidents either are the product of the author's imagination or are used fictitiously. Any resemblance to actual persons, living or dead, events or locales is entirely coincidental.

Copyright © 2014 by Benjamin Holmquist

www.benjaminholmquist.com

Book design by Benjamin Holmquist

"The only way to deal with an unfree world is to become so absolutely free that your very existence is an act of rebellion."

-Albert Camus

PART I
THE CELL

Chapter One

The Cell. It's an appropriate name for a city that never sees the sun. I'm used to the darkness by now, but still unnerved by the ash that sometimes falls from the sky like snow. A cloud of the stuff blows across my path as I walk down Street J-43 toward my destination- a public water dispenser. It's one of the only safe ways to get water anymore, due to the aftereffects of the war. For the past three years, it's been the only legal way to get a safe drink. Ever since Day Zero, water and electricity have been nearly impossible to come by. I'm lucky if the lights work for twenty minutes out of the day. The only places that always have power are city squares and The Spire, the massive dark tower in the middle of the city.

As I turn the corner into the small square where water is dispensed, the smell of smoke that permeates every corner of The Cell becomes stronger. I look up to find a line of at least fifty people, each one holding some sort of water jug. Removing my own bottle from my overcoat, I walk past two Faceless, who are guarding the end of the line. We're told they're here to watch over and protect us, but the masked guards seem to invoke more fear than comfort in the vast majority of citizens. Dressed from head to toe in black armor and carrying clubs, they wear full face masks displaying the emblem of The Dominion: a red letter D encompassed by a white circle. To The Dominion, it's a symbol of order. To everyone else, it's the sign of suppression and tyranny. If anyone speaks to another person in the street, the Faceless could drag them off to jail. If you're caught breaking curfew, chances are you'll be dragged off to The Spire and punished accordingly.

It hasn't always been this way. Thirty years ago, mankind took what was once a beautiful land and destroyed it. What had once been a land of forest and lakes, rivers and meadows has been turned to a barren wasteland. Ash and smoke cover the sky, and they say that no one has seen the sun in thirty years.

I'm forced from my thoughts by the deafening, metallic alarm that signals curfew throughout the city. All around the square, people are looking at each other and checking their watches, confused. Curfew isn't until nine, and it's barely five. Before the Faceless can react to the murmuring crowd, a large video screen on the side of the square comes to life. The familiar emblem of The Dominion appears, and the video cuts to the image of a pale man with jet-black hair.

He is known only as Blackthorn, and he's in charge of everyone in the city. The stories say that in the months following Day Zero, Blackthorn had been a kind, well meaning survivor who took the weak under his wing and provided protection. People looked up to and trusted him, and he soon emerged as the obvious leader of the survivors. His good looks and charm earned him the respect and power he so desired.

But power can far too easily corrupt a person. As the months and years went by, Blackthorn began to show himself to the people less and less, preferring to watch over the city from his throne in The Spire. He began building a close group of followers, who would soon become the first members of The Dominion, Blackthorn's ruling council.

A massive wall, over three hundred feet high, was built around the entire city. They say it's to keep out radiation from the war, but it seems to be keeping the citizens in more than anything. I've been around the wall at least a hundred times. No doors, no stairs, and hundreds of Faceless patrolling around the top. For now, citizens of The Cell are trapped, with no idea what lies outside.

I turn my attention back to the screen. Blackthorn begins to speak in a low, soft drone, revealing uneven yellow teeth.

"Due to a number of collapsed workers in factories eight and nine, curfew has been moved to six pm. This will allow citizens to acquire more sleep and contribute their fullest efforts to the advancement of our city." He pauses. "After all, a hand cannot function unless all the fingers are properly united. Any citizen found outside their home between the hours of six pm and eight am will be dealt with as the arresting guards see fit."

Blackthorn's sallow image is replaced with the words END TRANSMISSION and the emblem of The

Dominion before the screen goes black and the street lamps come back on. All around the square, people's fear and confusion can be seen in their faces. I know the same scene is unfolding in every other square in the city. Most of these people probably work in the factories. As people scurry around, trying to get back to their homes before a Faceless pins them for breaking curfew, I approach the grizzled attendant at the water fountain.

"One gallon, please." I hand over my bottle. As the old man fills it, I turn my gaze toward The Spire, towering over the city in the distance. It must be at least 150 stories tall. I can see the sign of The Dominion at the very top, just visible through the clouds of ash. Inside that tower, deep within the dark walls, are all those who have broken the law. It's also the home of The Faceless, and the location of Blackthorn's throne room- which I've only ever seen on video.

My gaze returns to the ground as the attendant hands me my water.

"That'll be thirty-seven fifty."

I reach into my pocket and withdraw two folded and worn bills. As he reaches into a brown leather bag for my change, the man's black eyes seem to look right through me.

"You be careful out there, son."

I nod and accept my change. Turning around, I make my way across the cobbled stone floor toward the street that will lead me home.

Chapter Two

I suppose I should start by talking a little bit about myself. My name is Noggin. I don't have a last name, or at least not one that I know of. People gave up formalities like that long ago, instead choosing to focus on other things- like surviving. I'm seventeen years old, and I live with my parents and my younger sister, Flora. She's twelve. My father works long hours at a factory in the heart of the city, and my mother stays at home, taking care of the cooking and cleaning. We all live together in a three room apartment, on the first floor of an abandoned warehouse. It's not much, but we're lucky to have a place to live in such dangerous times.

My father has told me stories of a different world, long ago. He can remember a time when people weren't constantly living in fear. It seems hard to imagine now, with the emblem of The Dominion plastered everywhere, but I believe my father. Sometimes I wish he'd be around more, but he's gone all day for a reason- to provide the best living he can for our family.

Suddenly I hear something behind me. From around a corner, two men emerge, out of breath from running. They pause to catch their breath, hands on their knees, and then take off again- right toward me. Hoping they'll just go around, I stand still. But the first man barrels straight into my shoulder, knocking me to the ground.

I climb up onto all fours and grab my water jug. Luckily it's still full and in one piece. I look up to see the two men running down the alley, under the light of two street lamps. Their feet suddenly appear to catch on something unseen, and both of them fall forward onto their faces.

I feel the slightest of breezes pass by, and in the blink of an eye there is a dark figure walking quietly past me toward the two men. The figure's footsteps are absolutely silent. The only sound is the almost indecipherable breeze as it passes by. The two men look up, and the look on both their faces is undoubtedly one of pure terror.

This mysterious person is dressed in all black- from the hooded face, to the tight black pants, down to the leather boots. The figure approaches the men, and moves into the light of the streetlamp. The two men start whimpering.

"Please! Just leave us alone!"

"Take our money! Take whatever you want! Just let us go!"

The figure removes the dark hood, and I get a glimpse of a young man with jet-black hair and a sharp face. He speaks in a soft but intimidating voice.

"That's exactly what I plan on doing tonight, boys."

The men exchange a worried glance.

The mysterious young man speaks again. "Hand it over."

One of the two men on the ground finds some confidence, and snaps at the visitor. "You're nothing but a common thief!"

The man in black laughs. "Oh, is that all I am? Why don't you tell that to the hardworking family you stole those bags from?" He glances pointedly at the bags, strewn across the alley. "I plan on returning those to their rightful owners."

I catch my breath. Maybe I won't be witnessing a murder tonight after all. The man in black picks the two bags up off the ground, and puts them over his shoulder.

"One more thing," he says. "Next time you steal, don't do it in front of another thief- especially one with morals, like me." He jumps up onto the dumpster at the end of the alley, and looks down at the two thieves, pulling his black hood back on. As he prepares to jump over the fence and be on his way, he looks back. I catch a glimpse of piercing blue eyes, and the mysterious young man nods to me ever so slightly. Then he's gone, leaping over the fence into the darkness beyond.

It takes me a minute to catch my breath, but I finally do. The two robbers have run off into the darkness after the honorable thief who stole their stolen goods. I stumble back out onto the main road, and continue toward home.

Chapter Three

As I walk, I look up at the red digital clock on one of the non-working lamp posts. It's 5:55 PM- almost curfew. I quicken my pace, and soon I'm opening the door to my apartment. My mother greets me with a smile as always, even though she is clearly tired.

"Oh, Noggin. It's you. Did you happen to see your father out there?" she asks nonchalantly, although the nervousness in her voice is unmistakable.

"No," I reply, "but I got the water. Why? Is Dad in trouble?"

"I'm sure it's nothing," she says. "He was running

late for work this morning. I hope the new curfew doesn't get him into any trouble with the Faceless."

"I'm sure he'll be fine," I reply. "You know Dad."

"I'm sure you're right," she says. "I just can't help but worry. These are dark times."

I nod, and set the bottle of water on the counter by the sink. I roll up my sleeves and start washing the dirt and grime off my hands. My mother calls my sister.

"Flora, dinner's ready!"

Flora comes running into the room, her blond pigtails bouncing up and down on her shoulders as usual. She always seems to have a smile on her face; she's too young to know how terrible the world is. She takes her place at the table next to my mother, and I come over and join them.

"Where's Dad?" Flora asks, looking up at me with the wide brown eyes that everyone in our family has. I exchange a glance with my mother.

"He'll be home soon," my mother assures her.

"I hope so!" Flora says. "He's never around!"

"Your father does his best to provide for us, sweetie," my mother replies. "That's why he-"

She's interrupted by a knock at the door.

"Oh, is it locked?" Flora asks.

"It shouldn't be," I say. "That lock hasn't worked in a while."

My mother walks over and opens the door, and my stomach drops. Standing there are two Faceless, holding my father between them. His nose is broken, and his face is covered in blood. My mother gasps.

I stand up. "What's going on?"

The two Faceless shove my father into the room with such force that he stumbles into the table and knocks it over. Dishes go everywhere.

Flora and my mother run to my father and begin looking him over frantically. I turn to the Faceless.

"What's this about?" I ask. The Faceless stand there silently and don't respond. I raise my voice. "My father's done nothing wrong!"

"Actually, that's not entirely true." The voice comes

from outside, and a man walks into view from the dark street. He's dressed in all black like the Faceless, but his face is uncovered. His greying hair is slicked back, and he has dark shadows under his eyes. On his chin is a wispy looking goatee. He pulls an official looking document out of his coat pocket.

"This is an official search warrant for your house. We've received word that this family is involved in a conspiracy against The Dominion."

I take a step forward. "What did you say?"

"You heard me correctly, son." The man steps forward, and I can see every wrinkle in his face and almost taste the rotten fumes coming off him. He has the air of someone who revels in every opportunity to abuse their power. He holds up the document for me to examine, and I snatch it from him while maintaining eye contact.

My father is lying on the kitchen floor, while Flora and my mother tearfully try to stop the stream of blood pouring from his nose. "This is ridiculous," my mother sobs. "He needs medical attention!"

At a nod from the bearded man, the two Faceless grab Flora and my mother and roughly throw them across the room, into a corner.

"Who are you?" I ask. The man doesn't respond. I clench his search warrant in my hand. "You can't do this!"

On the floor, my father props himself up. The blood from his nose has crusted horribly on his face, but his voice is steady.

"Gentlemen, your business is with me. Leave my family out of it."

The bearded man chuckles and leans down so that his face is level with my fathers.

"Oh, Jonathan. You've been such a good worker in the factory. And you'll serve us even better once we find out what you're up to."

"What's going on? Up to what?" I interject.

"Silence!" snaps the bearded man. "Your father has committed crimes that can only be dealt with at The Spire. You all need to come with us."

"No one's going anywhere!" shouts my father, and

Flora starts crying again. I look over and see that my mother's face is wet with tears as well.

The man leans in close to my father's ear, and I can barely hear him whisper.

"If you don't come with us right now, I will kill each and every member of your family while you sit there and watch."

My father spits a mouthful of blood into the man's face. "You leave my family out of this, you bastard."

The man stands up and calmly wipes the blood from his face. I can see that beneath his calm exterior, he is filled with rage.

"Leave your family out of it?" He pauses and looks around, from me to my mother to Flora. "Maybe you should have done that yourself."

He pulls a long knife from his belt. My mother and Flora scream, and I jump forward, but it's too late. The man plunges the knife into my father's chest. I grab him around the neck and try to pull him off, but his fist catches me in the jaw and I spin backward, my face throbbing and my vision blurred.

The man drives the knife into my father's chest again before pulling it out and standing up. "Let's go! Bring these three. Let's get them to The Spire before this gets out of hand!"

My mother and Flora are putting up one hell of a fight. They're kicking and screaming, and the Faceless are having a hard time getting anywhere. The bearded man is out in the street, where a crowd has started to gather. All these people are breaking curfew, and more and more Faceless are starting to arrive to deal with the rule-breakers.

I see my chance and I take it. My father is barely stirring on the floor, but as I approach he opens his eyes and grabs my hand.

"Noggin." His voice is weak, and I have to lean in to hear what he's saying.

"Noggin. You need to protect your mother and sister." He coughs, and a fresh trickle of blood runs down his chin. "Promise me you'll do whatever it takes. Family is the only thing we've held on to in this world." The patch of red on his shirt is growing larger by the second.

"Hold on, Dad," I say, and I try to prop him up. He stops me with a weak raise of his hand.

"No, son. You're wasting time. Get out of here or they'll take you too."

I can hear shouting outside, growing stronger. It's only a matter of seconds before the Faceless come back in for me. My father's voice is growing weaker.

"Go out the side door, and get away while you can. You'll find a way to rescue your mother and sister. I know you will."

"I can't do this, Dad," I reply.

He looks me in the eye. "You have to, son."

A crash at the door forces me to look up, and the two Faceless are back. I glance quickly down at my father. He's gone. I leap to my feet, and thinking quickly, grab a chair from by the table and throw it at the Faceless. It catches them by surprise and they struggle around it as I dart out the side door and sprint down the alleyway.

Chapter Four

I rush down the alley, away from my house and what now sounds like a full-blown riot taking place outside. There are now at least fifty people there, shouting insults at the guards and throwing things. I find myself running aimlessly through the backstreets, and the sound eventually fades as I round several corners. After a while I slow my pace and consider what has just happened.

My father is dead. My mother and sister have been taken by The Dominion. And for what? If my father was involved in a conspiracy against Blackthorn, I had no idea.

Ever since I was young, he had always been there for me. When I was a baby, he would sit with me when I couldn't sleep so my mother could get some rest. The man worked fourteen hour days at the factory even then, so that couldn't have been easy for him.

When I was Flora's age, he would always have time to play games with me in the evening. We always had food on the table, which my parents constantly reminded me wasn't the case for a lot of families. And we kept no secrets from one another. I can't believe my father could be involved in anything like that, not when all he ever did was try to protect us.

None of that matters now. All I know is that I have to get my mother and sister out of the hands of The Dominion- and I have no clue where to start. Chances are, they are being taken to The Spire to be tortured until they reveal information about my father that they don't know.

My foot splashes into a puddle of water. I haven't been paying attention to where I walk, and now I have a foot full of water to pay for it. I sit down on a nearby bench to drain the water out of my shoe.

As I remove my old and worn boot, I look down into the puddle at my reflection. My reddish-brown hair is getting longer, although it's not quite to my shoulders. My father and I had that in common- neither of us liked getting haircuts. My mother always told me that in her day the ladies would swoon over hair like mine. I guess it's a different time now, because no one ever even makes eye contact with me. No one ever makes eye contact with anyone.

I finish putting my boot back on and walk over to the abandoned building on the other side of the puddle. When I was a kid, I used to climb onto the roof of this building to look out over the city and dream of flying over the walls. The drain pipe has a harder time holding me now, but I still make it to the top.

I sit down on the flat roof and look out over the city. Everyone calls it The Cell, but from up here it doesn't look quite so bad. In the distance, I can see The Spire towering above all the other buildings. The windows are all brightly lit, but I'm too far away to see anyone moving inside. The massive walls of the city are just visible in the distance, tall, black, and menacing.

I think about my next move. Time is of the essence, because the longer I wait to go after Flora and my mother, the longer The Dominion will have to torture them. Assuming they're still alive.

I shake the thought from my head. I can't afford to think like that. All that matters is finding them, because they're the only people I have left. I think back to my father's dying words. Promise me you'll do whatever it takes. Family is the only thing we've held onto in this world.

A light breeze rolls by and blows my hair into my face. I turn my head as I brush it away. That's when I see him.

The mysterious thief from the alley is staring at me from the roof of the next building over. He's sitting there silently, with his legs hanging over the edge. For some reason- I don't know why- I can tell that he recognizes me from earlier.

I open my mouth to voice a greeting, but before I can form the words the thief has leapt down from the roof and into the alley below. I rush over to the edge and see him walking silently down the dark street. He moves with a careless elegance that manifests both authority and rebelliousness, and suddenly, I realize what I have to do. I climb down the drainpipe and hurry after the shadowy figure.

Chapter Five

My mother always used to tell us legends of long ago. One of my favorite stories was about how before the war, people would hunt animals and kill them for food. I've never seen an animal in real life, of course, but the thought of capturing your own food was appealing to me. I can imagine the exhilaration of being responsible for your own meal- if you can't capture it, you can't eat it. I guess a person really had to earn their meal in those days.

One part of hunting I always knew I wouldn't be good at was the part where you quietly approach the animal. Even now, I can tell that my footsteps are making too much noise as I walk down street after street behind this mysterious thief. He's moving quickly, but I'm able to keep him in my sight as we travel further and further out of the city, toward the towering wall.

The thief makes several turns, sometimes even doubling back to take another street altogether. I'm struggling to keep up now. In this part of the city, the buildings are decrepit and abandoned. No one lives here, with the exception of a few homeless people who are nowhere to be seen tonight. Electricity never makes it this far into the outskirts of the city, so the night is darker than usual. I can barely see the thief in the darkness ahead of me.

Just when I think I'm about to lose the shadowy figure, a scraggly looking homeless man stumbles out of an alley to my right. His beard is matted and grey, and his brown coat is filled with holes. His voice has an eerie rasp to it.

"Help me!" He stumbles up to me and tries to grab my hand. "Help me! They're after me!"

I back away. "Who's after you?"

He doesn't seem to hear me. "They'll kill me!"

I hear footsteps approaching. As much as I want to help this poor soul, I have to rescue my mother and sister, and I can't afford to get mixed up in anything. I back away, looking around for the thief. He's nowhere to be seen.

Two men come out of the alley, and they're

carrying bats. I immediately recognize them as the robbers from the alleyway. What is going on here? I crouch behind a dumpster around the corner and watch.

One of the robbers punches the homeless man in the stomach and throws him to the ground, and then they both start hitting him with the bats.

"You think you can just steal someone's coat like that?" bellows one of the robbers. "You better learn your place, filth!" They continue beating him.

I look around for the mysterious vigilante. Isn't this the type of thing he should be stopping? But by this time it's too late. The homeless man is lying on the ground, unmoving and beaten to a pulp, and the two robbers have their coat back and are running away down the street.

When I'm sure they're gone, I come out from behind the dumpster and approach the victim. I crouch down to see if he's breathing. He's not- which is no surprise because his windpipe has been shattered.

"There's nothing you could have done." The voice comes from behind me, and I spin around to see the thief standing there, hooded and mysterious.

"I didn't even hear you coming," I say, but he doesn't seem to hear me.

"Is this justice?" he asks, seemingly to himself, as he walks around the body, looking down at it. "Did this man deserve to die? He was, after all, a thief. He had no doubt killed before. But does anyone ever really deserve to die?"

I don't have a good answer, so I stay silent. We stand there for another few minutes, until the man in black breaks the silence.

"You were following me," he says. It's not a question.

"Yes," I say hesitantly.

"Why?" he asks.

I choose my next words carefully. "I saw you in the alley earlier with those two men."

"And are you here to bring me to justice?" He removes his hood, and jet-black hair cascades down over a pale forehead. "Those men stole from hardworking families. I returned the items to their rightful owners."

"You are the one who brings justice, not me," I reply. "I need your help."

He laughs softly, and turns away. "Of course you do," he whispers. "You and eight million other people in this city."

"Please," I say.

"Forget it, kid," the vigilante says. "It's The Cell. Sooner or later, everyone gets what's coming to them."

I stand there, not knowing what to say as he puts his hood back on and disappears into the black night.

Chapter Six

I stand there for a few minutes before coming to my senses. I can't give up this easily. With every second that passes, Flora and my mother are getting closer to The Spire. For all I know they could be there already, tied to chairs with knives at their throats.

I run after the vigilante, but as I turn the corner the outer wall of the city appears in front of me. I hadn't realized how close to the edge we were. My house must be five miles from here. I look up, and see the faint outline of a figure in black climbing the wall. He must be at least fifty feet up. After a few seconds, I can no longer see him.

I find a nearby bench and sit down. I'll need to plan my next move carefully. I sit on the bench for several minutes, trying to decide how to proceed. The wall stretches up far into the darkness, with no end in sight. There must be some sort of cave or ledge up there where the hooded figure is hiding.

I walk over to the wall and examine it. The surface is smooth, black rock. There don't seem to be any footholds or anything that would allow me to climb up. I scour the wall carefully, and after a few minutes of searching I notice a small piece of rock jutting out. It's several inches beyond my reach, but it looks about the right size to hold onto.

I jump, but I can't reach it. I find myself wondering how in the world this mysterious vigilante was able to get up there. I look around and notice a wooden box in the entryway of a nearby building. It's the right size. I hurry over and grab it, placing in at the foot of the wall.

Now I can reach the rock! I grab it and pull myself up, but I can't find another handhold and I lose my balance. I fall down onto the cold, hard ground. It's quite painful, but I remind myself that my mother and sister are probably going through much worse right now.

Lying there on the ground, I realize I have no idea what I'm going to do. This mysterious vigilante is my only hope for rescuing my family. Without him, they're as good as dead- I can't do this alone.

"Are you up there?" I shout. "I really need your help! I just want to rescue my mother and sister." There is no response. "Don't you have a family? Wouldn't you want to do the same for them?"

The night air is absolutely still. I shake my head to myself. It was a long shot, anyway. I turn around and start heading back toward the city.

A breeze, ever so light, crosses the alley behind me. I stop, and hardly dare to breathe. Slowly, I turn around.

He's standing there, face obscured by the shadows.

"I have a sister," the vigilante says, stepping forward. "Or I did." He extends a hand.

I shake it. "I'm Noggin."

"Pleased to meet you, Noggin. Now let's go rescue your family." He strides briskly forward, and I quickly run after him.

"Wait," I call out. "Who are you?"

He stops and turns slowly, and the darkness of the alley makes him look even more menacing. "You can call me Shadow."

Chapter Seven

As Shadow and I walk down the dark empty street, I find myself feeling optimistic for the first time tonight. Shadow is a thief, a creature of the night, and maybe, just maybe, he can help me get my mother and sister out alive.

"So what happened to your family?" he asks as we walk.

"They were taken by the Faceless," I say. "The

Dominion thinks my father was involved in a conspiracy. They killed him, and they took Flora and my mother."

"Let me guess, they tried to take you too, but you fought back," Shadow interjects.

"Yeah," I say. "How'd you know?"

"I saw the whole thing," he says. "I was in the crowd out front. I left when things started getting heavy, and followed you until you noticed me."

"You were behind me that whole time?" I ask.

He nods.

"Wow," I say. "That's impressive. But why?"

He shrugs. "I wanted to see how you'd react to having your whole life ripped apart. It changes people. I wanted to make sure I wasn't going to have another vigilante to compete with."

"A vigilante?"

"Only half joking."

I'm not in the mood for jokes- not when my family is in danger. "Alright, let's get to The Spire. That's where they must be taking Flora and my mother."

Shadow pauses and puts a hand on my shoulder. "I want to make one thing clear, Noggin. If I'm to help you, we'll do it my way, with my team."

"Your team?"

"I know people who are very good at getting in and out of places without being noticed. Even better than me. There's no way you and I can do it alone, and since you've never done anything like this before, you'd likely get us both killed."

"Are you sure?" I ask. "Won't they be more likely to notice more people?"

"Trust me," Shadow says, and quickens his pace so I'm forced to jog in order to keep up.

We've been walking for a while now, and the cloudy sky is becoming a little brighter. I realize that it's morning. The sun never comes out, but the clouds aren't quite as dark as they are at night. We emerge into one of the large town squares, an almost identical copy of the one where I go for water. The only difference is that this one is abandoned. The large television screen on the side of the square is smashed beyond repair, and the water spigots are rusted and falling apart. Weeds poke through the cobbled stone floor.

"The Faceless don't come here," Shadow explains. "There's only one person who lives here, and he doesn't like visitors. But he's an old friend of my father."

Shadow leads the way up to a door in the side of one of the buildings. I hesitantly follow. The door is falling off its hinges, but Shadow knocks anyway.

After a minute, I hear a creaking sound coming from inside, and the door swings open to reveal the largest man I have ever seen. His shaven head sits atop a muscular frame, almost bursting through the t-shirt he somehow managed to fit into. He towers over me, nearly seven feet tall.

"What do you want?" The giant speaks in a thick accent that I've never heard before. He's chewing on a toothpick.

"Boris!" Shadow exclaims. "How are you? It's been so long!"

Boris stares at Shadow as if he doesn't recognize him.

"It's me!" Shadow says. "You and my dad used to work together."

I see the recognition appear on Boris' face.

"Shadow! How are you, my boy?" He grabs Shadow and wraps him in a powerful hug, which seems to make it impossible for Shadow to breathe. "Come in, come in!"

I follow Boris and Shadow into the building. It's not exactly a house, but rather a warehouse that Boris seems to have made into a cross between his living quarters and a workshop. One corner holds a bed and table, and a workbench with several tools sits in the middle of the floor.

"Can I get you something to eat, boys?" Boris asks. "There's not much, but I'm sure I can scrounge up some bread or something."

"No thanks, Boris," Shadow says. "We're actually in a bit of a rush. I've got a favor to ask."

Boris leans on the workbench, picks up a wrench,

and starts tossing it from hand to hand. "Of course, of course. Anything for the notorious Shadow. You still carrying on your old man's legacy?"

Shadow doesn't seem to hear the question. "Noggin here is in a bit of trouble. His father was killed last night for suspected action against The Dominion."

Boris sets down the wrench and nods to me. "My condolences, kid."

"Thanks," I reply.

"His mother and sister were taken to The Spire," Shadow continues. "We need to get them out."

"And how do you think you're gonna do that?" Boris asks. He strides over to the window, through which The Spire is barely visible in the distance.

"With your help, we could get in," Shadow replies. "You know more about weapons than anyone I know. You've gotta have something they won't expect."

Boris chuckles. "Oh, I have many things The Dominion wouldn't expect."

"Can you do it then?" I ask. "Can you help us?"

Boris turns away from the window. "Course I can, boys." He turns to Shadow. "It'll be just like old times. You got a hacker? Let me guess, Data's helping you with that side of things?"

"I lost touch with Data a few years ago," Shadow replies. "I was hoping you could recommend a good hacker who's actually around."

"A hacker?" I ask. "What exactly is that?"

"It's a computer expert," Shadow says. "Computer equipment is almost impossible to come by these days. They usually have to steal it from The Dominion. A good hacker is essential in this operation- we need someone who can access every part of The Spire's security network via computer."

"And I know just the one," Boris says. He lights a cigarette and grabs his jacket off the back of a chair. "Let's go."

"Where does he usually hang out?" Shadow asks. "I feel like I'd have run into him if he operates underground."

"You won't find this hacker unless you go way, way further underground," Boris replies.

"Who is this guy? Why haven't I heard of him?" Shadow demands.

Boris chuckles. "Not him. Her."

Chapter Eight

Boris leads the way down a maze of streets and alleyways. He walks quickly, and while Shadow has an easy time keeping up, I'm out of breath before too long. We turn the corner onto a dark street, tucked between two tall buildings. It's chilly, since the midmorning grey of the sky doesn't quite reach us back here.

A set of stairs leads down to the basement entrance of a building. The place looks like some type of nightclub. I've seen them around the city before- they operate illegally after curfew. Why anyone would be here this early in the morning is beyond me. Boris raises his large fist and knocks.

Shadow has his hands in his pockets, and I can

faintly see my breath in the crisp air.

"Are you sure this hacker will be here?" Shadow asks. "Seems like the type of place that doesn't open until later."

I look around, and on the wall I see a neon sign that's either turned off or broken. The words ELECTRIC LIGHTNING are elaborately scrawled in red, with a yellow lightning bolt slashing through the middle. This must be the name of the nightclub.

"She'll be here," Boris says. "If I know her, she'll be here."

The door opens just a crack, and a short, heavyset man pokes his head through. "We're closed."

"We have business with someone who works here," Boris says in his thick accent. "It's a matter of urgency."

"Sorry, chief. Come back at seven tonight. That's when we open."

"Looks like you're opening early today," Boris says, and kicks in the door. The short man goes sprawling across the floor, but picks himself back up quickly.

"You can't be in here!"

Boris ignores him and walks into the middle of the room, looking around. On one side of the room is a bar, underneath another sign advertising the club.

"Did you hear me?" The man is getting angry. "You can't be in here! I'm calling the authorities!"

"You and I both know you won't do that, my friend," says Boris. "Not at an illegal operation like this. I don't have time to waste, so I'll leave it up to you. We can do this the easy way, or the hard way."

"No. We're not doing this at all," the man snaps back.

Boris sighs. "The hard way it is." He grabs the man by the neck and slams him up against the wall. "I'm looking for a girl who works here. About 5'7". Really good with computers."

"I don't know what you're talking about," chokes the man. "I run this place on my own."

"Oh yeah?" asks Boris. "How do you explain that?" He nods at an elaborate computer system sitting on a platform on the other side of the room. "I know there's no way you're running that rig by yourself. Where is she?"

"Put me down!" screams the man, in a last ditch effort to win the fight. "It's just me here!"

The door behind the bar swings open and Boris' reply is cut short. A girl with bright green hair walks into the room. She freezes.

Boris turns back to the heavyset man. "Thanks." He drops him to the ground.

I turn my attention to the girl. She's strikingly beautiful, with bright green hair styled into elaborate spikes. Her ears have more piercings than I've ever seen, and she's even wearing a ring in her nose. I estimate her to be about twenty-five years old.

The girl walks around from the back of the bar. She's wearing a skin-tight leather outfit with black boots. She jumps up and sits on top of the bar.

"What'd he do this time?" she asks.

Boris, Shadow and I exchange nervous glances, but before any of us can respond the girl speaks up again.

"Wait a minute! Boris, is that you? What are you doing here?" She jumps off the bar and runs over to hug him. He returns the hug with his huge arms.

"It's good to see you again, Jade. We need your help."

"Somebody always does," she jokes. "Who are these guys?"

"This is Noggin and Shadow," Boris replies. "We have an operation that I think you'll be interested in."

"Let's head to my office," she says, and turns to the short, round man on the floor. "Don't let this happen again, Barry. Make yourself useful and clean up out here."

We follow Jade back behind the bar, and down a short hallway. On the door at the end of the hall she flips a switch, and presses her finger onto the door. A click sounds, and a green light shines from the door onto her eye. The door clicks again. I look at Boris and Shadow, who don't seem phased by technology that I thought only existed in The Spire.

Jade opens the door and walks through. We follow

her into a dimly lit room filled with computer equipment. Jade moves some wiring off one of the chairs, and gestures for us to do the same.

"Just put that anywhere. Now, what is it I can help you with?"

I realize that Boris and Shadow are looking at me, waiting for me to speak. I clear my throat.

"Last night, my father was killed for suspected action against The Dominion. The Faceless took my mother and sister, and I just want to get them back."

Jade leans back in her chair. "That's a rough night. Where did they take your family?"

"We believe Noggin's mother and sister are currently being held in The Spire," Shadow replies.

Jade looks from Shadow to Boris, and back to me. "So what do you want to do? Break into the most heavily guarded building in the city?" She laughs.

"That's exactly what we want to do," Boris says.

Jade laughs again, and then her smile disappears. "You're serious."

"Absolutely," says Shadow. "For every second that we sit around here, our chances of getting them out grow slimmer."

Jade pulls her legs up onto the chair. "It'd be suicide."

"Not with you on board," I say. "Boris says you're the best there is. If anyone can help us break into The Spire, it's you."

Jade turns to Boris. "Did you really say that?"

"It's true."

"When do you plan on doing this?"

"As soon as possible," I say.

She sighs. "Well, I'm in. I'll have to gather a few things if I'm going to help with this suicide mission. Let's meet at your place after curfew tonight, Boris. You're still in that godawful warehouse, right?"

Boris grunts, and she smiles. "Good. See you tonight, boys."

That's our cue to leave. Boris, Shadow and I walk out the door, past Barry the bartender and the empty bar, and back out into the street.

Chapter Nine

That evening at Boris' place, we're all silent. A small blaze burns in a fireplace at the edge of the room. Nobody speaks as we wait for Jade to show up. Boris is pacing back and forth, while Shadow sits in a dark corner by himself. I'm sitting in front of the fire, staring into the flames.

Twenty four hours ago, I watched my whole life collapse in front of me. Who knows what the next day will bring? I only just met Shadow, Boris, and Jade, and now we're going to break into the most heavily guarded building in the city together. Hopefully we can get my family out quickly.

I'm forced from my thoughts by a knock at the door. Boris opens it, and Jade walks in wearing a backpack, which she sets on the table. Shadow and I walk over and join them, and Boris lights a candle.

"So I guess we're really doing this," Jade says as

she takes off her leather jacket, revealing a black tank top underneath. "I mean, I guess if you're stupid enough to try breaking into The Spire, you're stupid enough not to back out."

"I just want to get my family back," I say.

"I know, kid," she says. "If I had a family, I'd feel the same way."

"I'm sorry."

"Ah, don't be," she replies. "Never knew 'em, so I don't miss 'em. Barry raised me, but he had more of a tough love approach. Now it's me keeping him in line- and he pays me to run the lights at his club. Strictly professional."

"We should get this started," Shadow says. "We're wasting time. Show us what you've got, Jade.

"You got it, boss." Jade opens her bag and pulls out a laptop computer. She turns it on. "I have maps of every building in the city on here, except The Spire."

"But that's the one place we need to go," I say.

"Give her a minute," Boris interjects.

Jade nods and brushes a lock of green hair behind her ear. "It's going to be tough, but if we can get to the security panel in The Spire I can access the map from there."

"And how will we get there?" I ask.

"The security panel is most likely in the center of the tower, near the top," Shadow says. "They'd need to keep it away from the windows, and there are no buildings nearby that provide easy access to the top half. It's the safest place."

"But how are we going to get to the top of The Spire without being noticed?" Jade asks.

Shadow turns to Boris. "You still have that grappling gun my father gave you?"

Boris chuckles. "You think I'd throw that out if there was even the slightest chance I'd get to use it again? No way, man. Of course I still have it."

"A grappling gun?" I ask. "What's that?"

"That, my friend, is how we're going to get into The Spire," Shadow says.

Boris walks over into the corner and grabs a large case. He brings it over into the light and sets it on the table.

"I haven't used this bad boy in a while," he says. "But basically, if we go on the roof of a building next to The Spire we can use it to get across and break into a window."

"Seems kind of sketchy," I remark.

"Do you want to save your family or not?" Shadow demands.

"Of course I do," I say. "When do we start?"

Shadow looks at Boris, who turns to Jade.

"The best time would be around 3:30 AM," she says. "That way, everyone's asleep and we'll have enough time to get in and out before people start waking up."

"Security at The Spire will be minimal then," Shadow adds. "It's the ideal time."

I look outside at the clock in the square. It's almost 8:30 PM.

"We should get some sleep," Jade says. "You look like hell, Noggin. And we should all be well rested for a mission like this."

"She's right," Shadow says, and Boris grunts his agreement. We all find different corners of the room to curl up in, and before I know it I'm drifting into an uneasy sleep.

Chapter Ten

I awake several hours later to the sound of Jade zipping her backpack shut. Shadow and Boris are nowhere to be seen. I stand up and walk over into the light of the candle, which by now is burning low.

"Thought I was gonna have to wake you myself," Jade says as she grabs her jacket off the back of a chair.

"Where is everyone?" I ask.

"They went to scope out buildings around The Spire," Jade says. "We'll need to find one that will easily allow us to climb across."

I still can't believe we're going to do this, but I remind myself that I need to do whatever it takes to rescue my mother and sister.

Jade grabs her backpack. "Ready to go?"

I nod, and put my coat on. We exit Boris' house.

I've never seen the city so quiet or dark. The clock reads 3:26 AM, and there are no lights anywhere. I can barely see as Jade and I make our way across the cobbled stone square and into the street.

"So tell me about your mother and sister," Jade says as we walk toward the city.

"There's not much to tell, really," I say. "We were just an average family until the other night."

"How old is your sister?"

"Flora's twelve."

Jade smiles. "She's lucky to have a brother like you."

"Why do you say that?"

Jade looks at me. "Not everyone would try to rescue their family from The Dominion. I'd say you're not just an average family."

I shrug. "I'm just doing what I know they'd do for me."

"Like I said, no average family."

We fall into silence as we round a corner into the heart of the city. The Spire towers up into the sky, dark and menacing. I strain my neck, but I still can't see the top. The tower just disappears into the clouds of ash that always hang over the city.

Several buildings surround The Spire. They're still tall, but nowhere near the height of The Spire. Jade walks up to the door of an unmarked building. She pulls a complex looking tool from her back pocket, and begins picking the lock. A second later, the door swings open.

I follow Jade into what looks like another abandoned building. I'd never realized quite how many there were in the city. Jade sets her backpack on a table, and walks over to the front window.

"This is where they said they'd meet us," she says. "Let's hope they found a good place to break in- otherwise this plan is useless." She walks over and plops down at the table.

"I'm sure they will," I say. "Neither one of them

seem like the type to give up."

Jade nods her agreement, and we sit in silence for a while. After several tense minutes, Shadow appears at the door.

"We found the perfect place," he whispers. "But we've got to hurry!"

Jade grabs her things and the three of us head back out the door into the night. Shadow leads the way across the street, down an alley, and through the back door of a building directly next to The Spire. It's eerily silent as we start climbing the stairs toward the roof of the building.

We emerge onto the roof after seventy-five flights of stairs to see Boris fine-tuning the setup of his grappling gun. A long barrel is held up by a triangular metal piece, and a coil of rope sits on the back. He looks up.

"Did Shadow explain the plan to you?"

"Not yet," Shadow says. "I was waiting until we were all here."

"Alright, what do we do?" I ask. The adrenaline is pumping through my blood, and I'm wide awake despite the hour.

Shadow points across to The Spire, which is about fifty feet away from where we're standing, and addresses everyone. "We can cross here, and we'll be able to climb in on the 103rd floor. From what I've seen tonight, there are no guards within five floors of there. Once we're in, we'll be able to climb up and find the security panel. Then we'll be able to find the area with the holding cells, which is probably where Noggin's family is being held."

Jade nods. "All I need is five minutes with the security panel, and I'll have every nook and cranny of The Spire mapped out on my computer."

"Alright, let's do this," I say.

Boris turns to his elaborate gun, carefully lines it up, and pulls the trigger. A long rope with a claw at the end shoots out with amazing speed, up into the night. About twenty-five floors above us, it smashes through a window.

We all wait with baited breath for the Faceless to come running, but everything is silent. Boris tightens the rope, and the other end catches on something, forming a straight line up at an angle into the darkness. He hands everyone a pair of black leather gloves.

"These will help prevent blisters," he explains.

"Blisters?" I ask.

"Yeah, for when you're climbing across."

Shadow leaps up onto the ledge. "Whatever you do, don't let go. Or look down." He grabs the rope and starts pulling himself hand over hand, up toward The Spire.

I feel my stomach drop. We're seventy-five floors up. One mistake, and it's a long fall back to the ground. I make eye contact with Jade, and I can tell she's thinking the same thing.

"You're nervous, kid," says Boris. He puts a hand on my shoulder. "You'd be a fool if you weren't. But I'll tell you one thing." He looks me in the eye. "Just think about your sister. That's why you're doing this. It's bigger than you. And you realize that, kid. That's what I like about you."

Boris gives me a pat on the back and prepares to climb onto the rope. Shadow is already almost to The

Spire. I look at Boris, and he looks back and nods. He's a rough looking guy, but underneath he realizes what this is all about: family.

Chapter Eleven

Shadow reaches the end of the rope and climbs through the window. I see him looking around, and I realize that he has no idea where to go. Shadow knows this city like the back of his hand, but he's in unfamiliar territory now.

As soon as Shadow lets go of the rope, Boris grabs it. His huge arms carry him across with little effort, although I notice that the rope bends down quite a bit. When he reaches the other side, Boris has a harder time getting in. He struggles for a few seconds, and then pulls himself through.

Jade and I look at each other. Neither of us want to go next, but someone has to. It might as well be me. I step up onto the ledge, and despite Shadow's warning I immediately look down. Bad choice. The ground is several hundred feet away, and I find myself getting dizzy.

Jade steps up and grabs my arm. "You can do it, kid. It's simple. Just like Shadow said. Don't look down, and don't let go."

I swallow nervously and grab the rope. The leather gloves are tight on my hands, so at least I'll be able to hold on sufficiently. The gloves have a sticky leather material on the palms, which will make gripping the rope even easier. I turn to Jade one more time, and she gives me the thumbs up.

I take my feet off the ledge, and now I'm hanging by my hands. The Spire seems a lot further away now. I start pulling myself hand over hand along the rope. Jade calls out some words of encouragement, but I barely hear her.

What a ridiculous sight this must be. I think back to a week ago, before all this. It feels like a much longer ago. I was a normal kid- or as normal as anyone living in this twisted city can be. If I'd looked up and seen someone climbing a rope between two buildings, seventy-five floors up, I wouldn't have believed my eyes. Now here I am, taking part in this reckless camisado with three people I barely know. I remind myself that I'm doing this for my mother and Flora, and focus back on the task at hand.

I've never had tremendous upper body strength. Although I'm not out of shape, I'm definitely not used to holding up my entire weight with my arms. I look up and across at the window. Shadow and Boris are mouthing words of encouragement. It's a good thing they aren't yelling- the last thing we want is a guard in The Spire hearing us.

I'm about halfway across by now. It seems to be going pretty well, but I know better than anyone that things can change in the blink of an eye. I'm growing extremely tired from swinging myself hand over hand along the rope, but before I know it I'm three-quarters of the way across.

That's when my right shoe falls off. I must not have tied it tightly after I stepped in that puddle earlier. As I feel it slide off my foot, I instinctively look down. The ground is at least five or six hundred feet away. I can't see any people, but the streets look tiny. Five or six rows of barbed-wire fence wrap around the building. It's all I can do not to vomit as I watch my shoe tumble out of sight into the darkness below. It bounces of the wall and eventually hits the ground with a faint thud.

"You can do it!" Shadow calls out. "Come on!"

I use the last of my strength to pull myself up the remaining ten feet of the rope. Shadow and Boris help me through the window, and I collapse on the floor with my back to the wall. As I catch my breath, I can hear Jade making her way across the rope. It takes her a fraction of the time it took me, and she nimbly leaps through the window without any assistance.

I stand up and look around. A long hallway stretches out in both directions, dimly lit by red fluorescent lighting. A breeze comes through the window, a cold wind blowing ash and dust through the dark night above the city. I turn to Shadow and he nods. Boris and Jade turn and start examining the corridor. We're in.

PART II
THE SPIRE

Chapter Twelve

The hallway seems to stretch on forever. Red lights dimly illuminate the corridor as we carefully move away from the window.

"Where do we go from here?" I whisper. "We can't just stay out in the open like this."

Shadow nods. "There's bound to be a patrol of guards eventually. We should try and find the security room as soon as possible."

"It'll be up a few floors," Jade says. "This just looks like a maintenance hallway. Thats probably why there are no guards."

She leads the way down the hallway. Our footsteps echo loudly in the pre-dawn silence, and I keep expecting the Faceless to come out of nowhere. The red lights flicker off and on, making this even more creepy. We walk in silence for a while, and the hallway curves slightly to the right.

"This must lead all the way around the outside edge of The Spire," Shadow says. "I never realized quite how big it is in here."

"Let's hope we don't have to find out," I reply.

When we finally reach the end of the corridor, a large door stands in our way. I turn the knob to no avail- it's locked.

Shadow puts a hand on it. "Reinforced steel. We're not breaking this one down."

"Damn." Boris cracks his knuckles disappointedly.

Jade laughs softly as she rummages through her black bag. "Classic Boris. What are you gonna do when I'm not there to pick locks for you?"

Boris chuckles. "What are you gonna do when I'm not there to stop thugs like that lowlife from the bar beating you up?"

Jade pulls a lock pick from her bag and shakes her head.. "Let's hope it never comes to that." She presses her ear to the door, and inserts the skinny metal device into the lock. We all wait with baited breath as she slowly moves the lock pick from side to side. After what seems like an eternity, the lock clicks open.

Jade mock bows. "Thank you, thank you."

"Let's go," Shadow says. "We need to find that security panel- and quickly."

Boris gives the door a push, and it swings open without a sound. We all file through and survey the large room ahead of us.

The floor is made of black marble. The room is dimly lit by minacious lights built into the walls. To the right, a row of five elevators sits waiting.

"Elevators," I say, surprised. "I've never actually been in one."

"No elevators for us," Shadow replies. "We'd be better off publicly announcing to Blackthorn that we're here. We'll take the stairs."

Jade leads the way to another door on the left side of the room. "They'll know we're here soon enough. We'd better hurry."

The stairs are made of the same black marble as the floor. It's a very intimidating surface- almost as if Blackthorn wants to remind everyone who enters The Spire who's in charge.

When we reach the next floor, Jade opens the door a crack. "This looks like a medical floor. Let's try the next one up."

We continue up the stairs. At the next door, one of the lights on the wall is out. In the darkness, Jade signals for us to keep quiet as she looks through the door.

"What do you see?" demands Shadow.

"It's the security floor, alright," Jade replies. "But we've got a problem."

"What's that?" I ask.

"There are three Faceless in the hallway. They're just standing there. It's almost as if they expect us to try and access the security panel."

"How could they?" I ask. "No one knew we were coming tonight."

"It's probably nothing," Shadow says. "There are hundreds of security panels in the building. Nothing special about this one, is there?"

Jade shakes her head. "They'll probably move

along soon. Let's just hope they don't come through here."

Shadow presses his ear to the door. "I can still hear them talking."

We all move into the gloomy corner of the stairwell.

"Good thing this light's broken," Jade whispers. "We might be able to stay hidden for a bit longer."

I'm starting to become frustrated. "We need to get to my mother and sister now," I whisper urgently. "Who knows what they're doing to them in here!"

Boris puts a hand on my shoulder. "Relax, kid. We'll find your family. But it's no use to them if we get ourselves captured, too."

"Sorry," I reply. "I just really want to find them."

"I know you do, kid. And when we do-"

Boris quickly falls into silence as the door opens. We all huddle together in the small corner of darkness with baited breath.

The three Faceless are marching down the stairs. A voice is coming from a walkie-talkie on on of their shoulders:

63

"...we'll need you to check it out. Probably nothing, but they requested a routine inspection in the area. Report back once you've cleared it."

The Faceless don't even glance into our direction as they walk down, but we don't dare to breathe until hearing the sound of the door close two floors below. Shadow immediately springs into action.

"We need to hurry! They must be headed to where we broke in. If they find that broken window, this whole place will go on lockdown and a spider couldn't even get in without them knowing."

We rush back up to the door. Boris opens it without hesitation, and we scramble into the security hallway. It's completely empty, and along the left side is a row of monitors, each displaying a different room in The Spire.

"Here!" Jade exclaims, gesturing to a door at the end of the hall. The others all run toward it, but I stand frozen in shock. The screens on the wall are all cycling through footage of different rooms, but my gaze is fixed on one in particular. On one of the screens, marked BLOCK

7-15, my mother and Flora are chained together in a prison cell.

Chapter Thirteen

"Noggin!" Shadow hisses. "What are you doing?"

I glance in his direction, afraid to look away from the sight of my mother and sister, afraid that they will disappear.

"Come on!" Shadow says urgently. I look back at the screen. It now reads BLOCK 7-16, and shows a different cell. I hurry after the others.

We're all crammed inside a tiny dark room. On one side is a low shelf, where Jade sets her backpack. On the other side, hundreds of wires and switches cover the wall. Jade goes to work, pulling her laptop out and examining the wires.

Shadow helps her while Boris and I keep an eye on the door.

"I saw my mother and sister on one of the screens out there!" I say. "They were chained up."

"Really?" asks Shadow. "Are you sure it was them?"

"Positive," I reply.

"What did the room they were in look like?" Boris asks.

"It was a prison cell, there wasn't really anything unique about it."

Boris shakes his head. "That doesn't really give us much to go on, kid. But at least we know they're alive."

I nod. "There was one more thing. On the side of the screen it said BLOCK 7-15. Could that be the number of their cell?"

"We'll see," Boris says. "More than likely. They have to keep track of them somehow." He turns to Jade and Shadow, who have connected several wires from Jade's computer to the bank of wires on the wall. "How's it coming, guys?"

"Almost there," Jade replies. "I just need to reconfigure the firewall, and…" She hits a button on her laptop. "Boom. We're in."

We all quickly look over her shoulder at her computer. A transparent three-dimensional model of The Spire is on the screen.

"This is where we are," Jade says, and zooms the image in on a section about two-thirds of the way up. "But the prison cells are all located underground. That's at least a hundred stories down, and it's probably where your mother and sister are, Noggin."

"Are they labeled?" I ask.

Jade nods. "They start one floor below ground, and continue all the way down to sub level twenty-five. From the looks of it, security gets tighter the further down you go."

I take a look at the map. The first sub level is labeled BLOCK 1. Sure enough, the seventh one down is labeled BLOCK 7. Several cells line the walls, each one labeled with a number.

"That's where they are," I say, and point at the cell marked with a 15. "That's where my mother and Flora are."

Shadow nods. "Let's hope that footage on the monitor was current."

"It's the best chance we've got," Jade says. "I don't see why they would have moved them." The others nod their agreement.

"How are we going to get down there?" I ask.

"Well, the only access is through the main elevator bank," Jade replies. "And there's no way we can use that. The Faceless would be on us in seconds. However, there is another way. But it'd be very dangerous."

Boris cracks his knuckles, and Shadow chuckles.

"We've made is this far," I say.

"I thought you'd say that," Jade continues. "The only other way in is through an abandoned elevator shaft that leads to the underground levels. It's been out of use for years, according to this." She gestures at her computer. "They sealed off all the entrances, with the exception of the underground ones. I guess they didn't think anyone would try to use it down there."

"How are we going to get to it?" Boris asks.

Jade points at another spot on the map. "This here is a floor that used to contain medical facilities. Doesn't look like anyone really goes through that area anymore, but the elevator door is still intact. We can get in through there."

"We'll have to hurry," Shadow says urgently. "Who knows when they'll discover that broken window."

Boris opens the door a crack. "It's all clear."

We tiptoe out of the room and back into the hallway. The monitors are all still on, cycling through footage from different security cameras.

"This way!" Jade whispers, and we follow her back toward the stairs.

"I'm coming, Flora," I whisper to myself as I hurry after the others. "I'll get you out of here soon."

I hope we can pull this off.

Chapter Fourteen

We burst through the door and back into the stairwell. Jade leads the way, laptop computer in hand.

"We need to go up five floors!" she says. "The elevator shaft will be on the opposite side of the building, so we'll have to cross over somehow."

"Shouldn't be too hard," Shadow points out. He checks his watch. "I don't think they'll have an unused medical hallway under heavy guard, especially at 4:30 AM."

"True," Boris says. "Plus, with all the Faceless-"

He's interrupted by the deafening sound of an alarm, echoing through the stairwell. We come to a halt. Bright red lights start flashing above all the doors, and a hidden loudspeaker comes to life.

"Attention. Initiate lockdown protocol immediately. We have received notification of an intrusion from outside. Report any unusual activity to your nearest guard immediately. Repeat. Initiate lockdown protocol."

The message continues to repeat itself in a metallic voice. We all look at each other, nobody daring to move.

"We need to get to that elevator shaft now!" Shadow calls out over the noise. "They could be locking it down as we speak!"

We hurry up the last few flights of stairs and through the door. The alarm isn't quite as deafening here, but it's still very loud. Shadow, Boris, Jade and I all lean with our backs to the door for a minute, catching our breath.

Jade consults her computer. "According to my calculations, the elevator shaft should be at the very end of this hallway on the left."

The hallway doesn't look very inviting. Jade was right when she said it wasn't likely that people came here very often. Flickering lights sporadically line the ceiling, and a few of the doors are eerily swinging on their hinges.

"Do you think there's anyone up here?" I ask, and Jade laughs.

"Not for a few years, by the looks of the place."

We start moving slowly down the hallway, and I peer into one of the side rooms as we walk by. It's empty, apart from a bed frame collecting dust. The wall cupboards are all open and empty, as if the room was quickly cleared out a long time ago.

An overturned gurney rests under one of the flickering lights, and we carefully step around it as we near the end of the hallway. There's no sign of an elevator.

"Where is it?" Shadow asks. "We're in the right place, aren't we, Jade?"

Jade looks at her computer screen. "Yeah, it should be right here."

It's difficult to see in the gloom of the hallway, but as one of the lights flickers I catch a glimpse of a clumsily boarded door a few yards from where we stand.

"Here it is!" I exclaim, and rush over. The others quickly join me. Shadow and Boris pull the boards off the door. They weren't nailed on very tightly, which seems strange. When all the boards are off, we step back and look at the door.

"There's no handle," I say.

"Leave it to me," Boris says. "Stand back!" He backs up and prepares to kick down the door.

"Wait!" Shadow interjects. "Look at this!" He puts

a hand in the middle of the door and runs it up to the ceiling. "Theres a small crack here. It must open from the middle."

"Is there anything we can pry it open with?" I ask, looking around.

"Here," Jade says. "Use one of these broken boards." She hands me one. The end is sharp from where it split when we pulled it off. I hand it to Boris, and he slides the sharp end into the small crack in the door.

After a few minutes of struggling with the board, Boris finally pries the elevator doors apart a tiny bit.

"Somebody grab it," he says. "I can't hold it like this for long!"

Shadow and I each grab one side of the door, and with some effort pull them apart enough to squeeze through into the elevator shaft.

"Careful!" Jade says, and pulls me back as I step forward. I look down, and realize that there is no floor ahead of me.

"Thanks, Jade," I say. "I didn't realize the floor

would be gone."

"It's an abandoned elevator shaft, kid," she replies. "Did you think it'd have a nice carpeted floor laid out just for you?" She rolls her eyes, but she's smiling.

Shadow is examining the elevator shaft. "There's a steel beam about twenty-five feet down that we could rest on," he points out. "We'd just need a rope to climb down with."

"I've got you covered there," Jade says. She pulls a coil of rope out of her bag and hands it to Boris.

Boris and Shadow tie the rope around two planks from the hallway and throw the other end down into the darkness. They jam the boards in between the two halves of the door, sufficiently supporting the rope.

"How long is that rope?" Shadow asks.

"About fifty feet," Jade says.

"Fifty feet?" I exclaim. "We have to climb down over a hundred stories!"

"We'll figure something out," Boris says. "Let's just get down to that ledge before we're seen."

Shadow goes first. He tests the rope by aggressively pulling on it, and then, satisfied with its strength, carefully lowers himself over the edge. Boris, Jade and I watch as he lowers himself into the darkness below.

A few minutes later, he calls up to us. "I made it! There's quite a lot of room to sit down here."

"I'm coming to check it out," Jade replies, and grabs the rope. She lowers herself down quickly, and before long it's my turn.

"You can do it, Noggin." Boris pats me on the back. "Much easier than when we climbed in. All you need to do is lower yourself down."

He makes a good point, and as I carefully climb onto the rope I realize that he's right. The only thing I really have to worry about is going too fast and burning my hands. Before too long, I'm at the ledge with Shadow and Jade. They help me find my footing, and I sit down, able to really relax for the first time today. In the impenetrable silence of the elevator shaft, the sound of the alarm is muted.

Boris is climbing down the rope.

"How are we going to climb the rest of the way down?" I ask.

"How about with that ladder over there?" Shadow points to a ladder on the side of the shaft, easily accessible from where we sit.

"What luck!" I exclaim. "Do you think it goes all the way down?"

"I'd be surprised if it didn't," Shadow replies. "Why else would it be there? Regardless, there's only one way to find out."

Suddenly, a loud crack fills the silence. Boris cries out and the boards holding the rope clatter down into the darkness below. His weight must have snapped them. I hurry over to the edge and look down. Boris is nowhere to be seen.

A pebble hits me in the head and I look up. Boris has miraculously managed to grab a handhold on the wall, about ten feet above us. As he calls out for help, I can see his grip slipping.

Chapter Fifteen

Shadow, Jade, and I all stand in shock, looking up at Boris.

"Hang on, Boris!" Shadow cries out. "We'll get you!"

"This isn't going to hold for long," he bellows back. "Get out of the way- I might fall on you!"

"No one's going to fall, Boris!" I shout. "Just hold on for a minute!"

"What are we going to do?" Jade asks. "He won't be able to hold himself up there for long."

Shadow nods. "Do you have anything in that bag of yours that might help?"

Jade grabs her bag and rummages through it.

"Here!" She pulls out another, shorter coil of rope. "Can we throw this up to him?"

Above us, Boris cries out again.

"We can try," Shadow says, and grabs the rope.

"Boris! Do you think you can catch this rope?"

"Does it look like I can do anything right now?" Boris grunts.

Shadow doesn't seem to hear him. "Alright. Noggin, help me tie this rope around the beam here. If Boris can grab a hold of the other end, he might be able to swing down."

Shadow and I quickly tie the rope around the steel girder beneath our feet. "That should hold," I say, testing the strength of the rope by pulling on it.

"It'll have to," Shadow says, and grabs the other end. "Boris! Grab the end of this rope!"

He tosses it up toward Boris, but the rope falls short by about two feet. Shadow tries again to no avail.

"It's not going to reach him," Jade says.

"What do you suggest?" Shadow demands. "He's not going to climb down, that's for sure!"

"There must be another way," I interject. "If we can just-"

Suddenly, with a bellow of surprise from Boris, the

narrow bit of rock holding him up snaps off. With nothing to hold on to, he drops from the wall.

"Grab the rope!" Shadow screams, and holds it out urgently. If Boris doesn't get a hold of this rope, he will fall hundreds of stories to his death. As Shadow holds the rope out, Boris reaches his hand toward it.

I'm watching from a few feet away. As if in slow motion, Boris grabs the rope from Shadow with one hand, and falls with it into the darkness below.

"Boris!" Jade screams into the void. "No!"

The rope tightens, but the knot that Shadow and I tied around the steel beam holds. I walk over to the edge, hardly daring to breath.

Twenty-five feet down, Boris is clutching the rope with both hands. I breathe a sigh of relief.

"You can't get rid of me that easily," he chuckles breathlessly, and starts climbing up the rope.

"Get him up," Shadow says, and with the help of Jade and myself, we soon have Boris up on the ledge with us.

"Alright," he says, brushing the dirt off his trousers with a massive hand. "How are we getting the rest of the way down?"

"There's a ladder on the wall," Shadow replies, pointing to it. "Hopefully it goes all the way down."

"Let's hope so." Boris walks over and looks at the ladder. "Seems sturdy enough." He looks at us. "Who's going first?"

"I will," I say, and step forward. The ladder is old, but it's still in good condition. The rungs are wide enough to comfortably hold two feet, but not too wide to hold. The first step seems solid enough, so I start making my way down the ladder.

The ladder descends downward into the shadowy abyss. With every step, I expect my foot to hit nothing but air, for the ladder to end and force us to find another way down. But it doesn't.

We climb down for several minutes, none of us saying a word. I'm in the lead, with Shadow right behind me, followed by Boris and Jade. As we descend into the inky blackness, I find myself wondering what we'll find at the bottom. Will my family be there? Will they be alive? And most importantly, will we be able to get them out of The Spire?

I won't give up until my mother and sister are out of danger. This is the promise I made to my father as he died, and I intend to honor it. I have to keep reminding myself that it was only a few days ago when I was living a normal life. Now I've broken into the heart of The Dominion with three people I just met, doing things I never thought I'd do.

My foot finally hits the ground as I step down off the ladder. The others quickly follow, and we all stand there, huddled together in the darkness of the bottom of the elevator shaft.

"What do we do now?" Jade asks.

"There should be a door on this wall somewhere," Boris says, walking over to the concrete wall. "I doubt they closed it off this far down. Keep in mind, we're seven floors underground right now."

I'd forgotten this fact, and I feel the claustrophobia

setting in as Boris and Shadow look for the door.

"Look!" Jade says. A faint shimmer of light appears through a crack in the wall. Boris and Shadow immediately start pounding on the wall where the light is coming from.

"It's hollow," exclaims Shadow. "This is the door!"

After a few minutes of pulling, we have the door open wide enough to fit through. We file out of the elevator shaft, squinting as our eyes adjust to the light.

Chapter Sixteen

We're standing on the edge of a massive room. The low ceiling is lit by hanging oil lamps, which cast a sinister glow over the scene. Hundreds of cages line the walls, each one containing at least one person.

"What's going on here?" Jade whispers as we move into the room.

"These must be all the prisoners they've captured," I say. "Jeez. They're treating them so horribly."

We walk down one row of cages. As we pass each

prisoner, they poke their heads between the bars and stare imploringly at us with starving faces. One woman with sallow skin, sunken eyes and thinning grey hair reaches out to Jade with a shriveled arm.

"Have you come to rescue us?" the woman asks, and I notice that her teeth are almost all gone.

Jade backs away, not knowing what to say.

"Please!" the woman cries. "I've been in here for eight years!" Her voice is a piteous wail, high and raspy.

Shadow and I look at each other. It's despicable what this place does to people.

"Let's try and get out of here as quickly as possible," I say.

Shadow nods. "Once we find your family, we should get back to the elevator shaft. We can hide there until the security breach blows over. Then we'll leave under the cover of night."

"Let's hope they don't find us before then," Boris puts in. "With this lockdown going on, it's a miracle we haven't already been discovered."

"How exactly are going to escape?" I ask. "We can't go back out the window where we came in."

Jade pulls out her laptop and points to a room on the second floor of The Spire. "This is a trash disposal unit. All the garbage chutes in the building lead to this room. There's a ventilation shaft there that leads out the back of the building. From the looks of it, security will be minimal at that point."

Shadow nods. "All we have to do is get past the guards and through the gate, and then we'll be free."

"Assuming the Faceless don't bring us right back in," I point out.

Shadow shakes his head. "We'll have to go into hiding. It's the only way to avoid being captured again."

"It's a big city," Boris adds. "Trust me, they won't find us."

"Oh, they'll find you," snarls a voice. I look over. It's a prisoner with a grey beard and an eye patch, gnarled hands clutching the bars of his cell. "There's no hiding from The Dominion, is there? No, sir!"

None of us say a word as he leers up at us, a stream of saliva trickling from his mouth.

"I'd get right out of here if I were you," he continues. "This place makes you go insane, I tell you!" He starts laughing manaicaly, a horrid gurgling sound.

"Come on," I say. "Let's find my family." I pull my gaze away from the hysterical old man and continue down the row of cells, the others close behind me.

"You won't find your family here, boy!" He calls after us. "This place changes people! Don't say I didn't warn you!" He falls back into that horrible laughter again, and it remains in my head even after we're out of earshot.

"Do you think my mother and Flora are alright?" I ask Shadow as we make our way past cell after cell of emaciated prisoners. "Everyone in here seems really messed up."

"I don't know." Shadow shakes his head. "These people must have been here for years. There's no telling what The Dominion does to them."

"These cells aren't labeled," Boris points out.

"There's no way of knowing where Block 7-15 is."

"They could be anywhere on this level," Jade says. "Should we split up and look for them?"

"That's a good idea," Boris says. "It'll save time. Noggin and Shadow, you go this way." He points to the left. "Jade and I will take the right. We'll meet up when one of us finds them."

Shadow and I take off to the left as Boris and Jade disappear in the other direction.

"They could be anywhere," I say as we quickly walk down row after row of cages. "There must be a thousand different cells here."

"We'll find them," Shadow says confidently. "They've got to be here somewhere."

"Flora!" I shout. "Flora! Can you hear me?" The only response is the mutterings of a multitude of prisoners.

Shadow and I turn a corner into the last row of cells.

I shake my head. "They must be on the other side. Let's go regroup with Boris and Jade." I turn to walk away.

"Wait!" Shadow grabs my arm. "Look."

I look up, and at the end of the row, in the last cage, my mother and sister are slumped against the wall, bound and gagged.

Chapter Seventeen

I can't believe my eyes as I run over to Flora and my mother. They're both in the same cell, with chains around their ankles. A heavy leather cloth in each of their mouths prevents them from talking, but as I rush over to them they scream against the material.

"Flora! Mother! You're alright!" I can barely believe what I'm seeing as I hug my mother and sister through the bars of the cage. "Here, let me get that out of your mouth."

I take the cloth out of Flora's mouth first, because she seems to be in the most discomfort. When I untie it, I notice that the rough material has left her face bruised and chafed. I clench my fist. The Dominion will have to pay for this, but now I'm just glad to be reunited with what's left of my family.

"Noggin!" squeals Flora as soon as she can speak. "What are you doing here?"

"I came to get you out," I reply, removing the restraint from my mother's mouth. "And that's exactly what I'm going to do."

"Noggin, this is insane!" My mother shuffles closer to the edge of the cage. "How did you even get in here?"

"I had the help of some new friends," I reply. "This is Shadow. Boris and Jade went the other way to look for you. They should be here any minute.

"It's a pleasure to meet you," Shadow says, approaching my mother and sister. "Noggin has said much about you. He was very insistent that I help with this operation."

"How are we going to get them out?" I ask. "There's no way we can break this door down, let alone get them out of those chains."

"I bet Boris will be able to figure something out," Shadow replies. "We shouldn't waste time. I'll go find him. You wait here."

Shadow dashes away down the row of cages, and I turn back to Flora and my mother.

"What happened?" I ask. "When they grabbed you. Tell me everything."

"It was awful," Flora says. "After Dad got- well, you know. They brought us outside. The man with the beard, he was their leader. And he was getting angry because people were gathering to see what was going on. They tied us up, and he yelled at the Faceless to go back inside for you. They rushed in, but I guess you slipped out the side door because they came back empty handed."

My mother nods. "We were so glad when we realized you'd escaped. The bearded man wasn't, though. He stabbed the two Faceless right there in the street when he found out you weren't there." A single tear rolls down her cheek. "After that, he called for backup and several more Faceless arrived. They dragged us to The Spire, and threw us in here."

"We haven't eaten since we got here," Flora adds.

"We were starting to think we'd never get out."

"Listen to me," I say, looking her in the eye. "I made a promise to Dad right before he died. I promised him that I would get you out of here. Both of you. And that's what I'm going to do."

"How are you going to do that?" My mother leans against Flora.

"My new friends are really good at getting in and out of places," I reply. "Jade- she's a computer hacker- found us an escape route. All we have to do is get you out of that cage." I look back down the row of cages. "Shadow should be back with her and Boris any minute."

"I'm really glad you came," my mother says. "When your father was stabbed, I started to think all hope was lost." She looks me directly in the eye, and her gaze is strong. "But you are most definitely your father's son, Noggin. Never forget that."

"Perhaps you'd like to join your father, Noggin," says a voice from behind me. I quickly spin around. The bearded man who killed my father is standing there, flanked by five Faceless. My heart sinks as I realize they are holding Shadow, Boris and Jade.

"Your friends put up one hell of a fight," the man says. He brushes a drop of blood from his nose with the back of a gloved hand and strokes his goatee. "But you can't fight The Dominion. It's high time you learned that."

I stand up. "Let them go!"

From the grasp of one of the Faceless, Shadow shakes his head sadly. He has a bloody scratch down his cheek. "Don't be a fool, Noggin."

I look at Boris and Jade, who are sporting similar injuries. Boris has a broken nose, and Jade has a scratch across one eye.

"At least we made it this far, kid," Boris grunts.

Jade nods. "I was glad to be a part of it."

"Shut up!" shouts the bearded man. "I won't hear any of this! You broke into the building and caused us a hell of a lot of trouble. Now, you must pay." He turns to the Faceless. "Grab the mother and the girl. Send them down to the lowest dungeon."

He turns to my mother and Flora. "You won't ever see the surface again where you're going!"

"No!" I shout, but one of the Faceless has already grabbed me roughly by the arms.

"And throw these pieces of filth into block nine." The man furiously runs a gloved hand through his goatee. "We don't want them getting any more ideas." He puts his face an inch away from mine. "And trust me, boy. Blackthorn will hear of this."

With that menacing statement, he turns on his heel and marches arrogantly away down the row of cages.

Chapter Eighteen

The Faceless march us down row after row of cages, randomly turning in various directions. I struggle against their hold, but the grip of the masked guard's black gloves is like iron. I can see Jade and Boris struggling from the corner of my eye, but Shadow, Flora, and my mother are all out of sight behind me.

"Why are you doing this?" Jade snarls to the

Faceless. "We've done nothing to you! What do you owe The Dominion?" The masked guards are absolutely silent. "Are you even allowed to talk?"

They don't respond, and Jade falls silent. After a while, the only sound is the footsteps of the Faceless, marching us to wherever it is we're going. I wonder to myself if we'll ever see the surface again. I alway took the dismal grey sky for granted. I often complained about the fact that it wasn't brighter. But now, I'd give almost anything to see that cloudy expanse again.

The Faceless abruptly turn us around a corner to the right. Up ahead, a dark stone staircase stretches down into the darkness, lit by a few torches on the walls. They start marching us down the stairs, and after a few flights we come to a stop. One of the Faceless wordlessly gestures to the right, at a wooden door. The door swings open from inside, and Shadow, Boris, Jade and I are brought over to it. As the Faceless roughly drag us through the door, I catch a glimpse of my mother and sister being dragged further down the stairs. Our eyes meet as the door closes behind us, and I hope to myself that it's not the last time.

We're being dragged past row upon row of cages that look exactly like the ones a few floors up. The prisoners in this block don't seem to have any reaction to us coming through. The Faceless are not gentle, and when we finally come to a halt at an empty cage they roughly throw us through the open door. I look up to see the bars close shut and the Faceless wordlessly walk away.

"Well, that's it I guess," Jade says. "We had a good run, fellas." She sits down on the floor in the corner of the cell.

"We can't just give up that easily," I say. "We'll find a way to get out! Won't we, Boris?"

Boris puts a massive hand on the bars. "This is reinforced steel, kid." He shakes his head. The only way we're getting out is with a key."

I slam my fist into the wall. "There has to be a way!"

A noise from down the row of cages causes me to run up to the bars. Two unmasked guards are approaching, wheeling a gurney between them on which a woman is tied down. Two Faceless march behind them, carrying clubs. The woman is bound and gagged, and seems to have given up whatever struggle she had in her. As they pass us, she tilts her head to the left and looks me in the eye. I have never seen a more hopeless person in my life.

The guards wheel the gurney through a set of red double doors that I hadn't noticed before. The doors swing shut behind them, and silence fills the air again.

"What was that about?" Jade asks.

"No idea," says Shadow. "Probably some kind of torture for the less cooperative prisoners."

"Let's hope it doesn't happen to us," I say.

"My guess is, it happens to everyone eventually," Boris says solemnly. "Those that live long enough, anyway."

With that thought, we all try to find a soft place to rest on the rocky floor. It's not comfortable by any means, but it'll have to do for now. I lie down on my back and stare up at the stone ceiling. With some difficulty, for the first time since we left Boris' warehouse, I fall into a restless sleep.

I couldn't tell you how long we are kept in the small cage. There's no way of telling what time it is, other than the fact that every twenty-four hours or so another bound and gagged prisoner is wheeled through the red doors on a stretcher. Every single one looks absolutely hopeless, as if they already know what will happen to them behind the closed doors.

This goes on for what must be weeks. A scruffy beard is growing on Boris' chin, and a thin layer of stubble covers his usually bald head. Shadow somehow looks almost exactly the same. My hair is down to my shoulders now, and I'm also sporting a beard.

We don't talk much. Most of our energy is spent trying to stay sane in the silence. When we talk it feels like a formality- just a way to remind ourselves that we're still alive.

Every day when the guards bring a new prisoner

past, I keep expecting it to be my mother or Flora. I always look up in anticipation when I hear them coming, hoping that it's not the sound of my mother or sister being brought in to be tortured. After a while, I stop bothering to look when the gurney goes by.

Chapter Nineteen

Boris and Jade are sound asleep on the other side of the cell. Shadow is leaning back against the wall, gazing into blank space. I haven't slept more than two hours in any given night for the past few weeks, and it's starting to take a toll on me. Combined with the severe lack of food we've been given, I'd wager that we won't last too much longer in here. Shadow seems to be thinking along the same lines.

"Do you think we'll ever get out of here?" he asks.

I shrug. "Who's to say? I'm just surprised they haven't tortured any of us yet."

Shadow pauses and tosses a pebble at the wall. "You're going through so much for your sister, and I hardly even got to know mine before she left."

"You never talk about that," I say. "Tell me about your sister."

"It's a long story."

"Does it look like we're going anywhere?"

He chuckles. "Fair enough. But I'll warn you now, it's a sad one."

I don't respond, so he continues.

"My sister was born when I was five or six, I don't exactly know. My parents named her Summer, after her bright blonde hair. I like to think they called her that because she was our light in the darkness. Those were the days when Blackthorn was first starting to form The Dominion, and things were going bad very quickly.

"Around that time, my parents were fighting back against Blackthorn. It wasn't quite a full-scale rebellion, but it was getting there. My parents knew that The Cell wasn't a safe place for a baby and a five-year-old, so they called upon a friend of theirs from the rebellion to take me and my sister out of the city."

I'm listening intently. I've never heard Shadow talk so much about his past, and I haven't heard much about the rebellion until now.

"The only problem was, this friend could only safely smuggle one child out of the city," Shadow continues. "They chose Summer. My parents' mysterious friend got her out, and we never saw either of them again. Five years later, my parents were murdered in front of me for suspected rebellion, just like yours. That was the end of whatever outright revolution might have started. I escaped and there I was, a ten-year-old kid, having to learn the streets of The Cell by myself. That's pretty much it. I met Boris along the way, and he helped me become what I am."

I'm fascinated. "I never knew that people fought back against The Dominion like that."

Shadow nods. "If Blackthorn hadn't had so many people killed, they would have likely been able to overturn his regime."

"That's too bad."

"You're telling me."

We fall into silence as Boris' snores fill the room. He's sleeping on the floor, at the edge of the cage. Shadow continues staring into the darkness, and I find a soft spot on the floor where I curl up.

So there was a rebellion. Was my father a part of it all along? I wouldn't put it past him. But it's still surprising. I drift into an uneasy sleep, with thoughts of revolution and captivity in my head.

I'm awoken a few hours later by the now all-too-familiar sound of a gurney being wheeled past. This time there are two of them. The prisoners are bound and gagged as usual, and two unmasked guards are wheeling them. Two Faceless walk along behind the others, clubs at the ready.

As this somber procession passes through the red door, one of the prisoners starts screaming and struggling. He's a skinny man, who looks as if he hasn't been fed in weeks- which I remind myself, he probably hasn't. He wears only filthy undergarments, and all his ribs are showing through his skin. Despite this, he puts up an admirable struggle. It takes both guards and one Faceless to hold him down.

"We've got to do it now!" shouts one of the guards mid struggle. "Let's get it done quickly!"

In their haste, they've forgotten to close the door. I shuffle over to the edge of the cell and peer through. The gurneys have been wheeled into a large room. In the center of the room is a chair, wired to a complicated looking piece of computer equipment. There are hand and feet straps on the chair, which the guards violently force the struggling prisoner into.

I look on in horror as the Faceless who isn't holding the prisoner hurries over to the computer and starts working the controls. When the poor man is sufficiently trapped in the chair, one of the guards nods. The Faceless presses a large button on the computer stand and an electric whirring sound pierces the air. I have to turn my head as the mans screams begin, panicked at first but soon reaching absolute agony.

This goes on for several minutes. When the screams finally stop, I look back hesitantly. What I see next stops my breath in my throat.

The tortured man stands up. There is no trace of the pain he felt a minute ago on his face. One of the Faceless brings over a bag, out of which the guard pulls a black leather outfit. He hands it to the man, who wordlessly puts it on. Then the guard pulls out another object. It's a face mask. The man puts it on, and with a sinking feeling I finally realize what happens in the red room.

They've been taking all the curfew-breakers, criminals, and outlaws and turning them into Faceless. This is how The Dominion keeps growing the forces of the Faceless. They're brainwashing people into serving them.

One of the guards notices that the door is open, and quickly runs over to shut it. I close my eyes and lean on the bars of the cell, hoping that he won't see me watching. He doesn't, or if he does he doesn't seem to care. After the door slams shut, I open my eyes and turn around.

Shadow is sitting there silently, eyes open. The

look on his face tells me that he saw the whole thing too.

"This changes everything," he whispers.

I nod. "My mother and sister could already be Faceless."

Shadow shakes his head. "We would have seen them taken into the room. Assuming it's the only one- come to think of it, there could be several more."

"So what do we do?"

Shadow takes a deep breath, and in the dim light of the prison cell he looks mysterious and intimidating. "We're going to get out of here. Tonight."

Chapter Twenty

Shadow and I shake Boris and Jade awake. It's not hard- they're sleeping about as well as I've been.

"What's going on?" Jade asks after seeing the urgent look on our faces. We all gather into a tight circle.

"We just found out exactly what happens in the red room," I say.

Their eyes widen.

"What? How?" Boris demands.

"There was a struggle with one of the prisoners," Shadow explains. "The guards forgot to close the door, and we saw the whole thing."

"And?"

Shadow sighs. "They're turning prisoners into Faceless, one by one. I don't know how they're doing it, the process involves some sort of strange electric mechanism, but it looks like they're brainwashing them."

Jade gasps, and Boris groans.

"Noggin's family is most likely still safe," Shadow continues. "We haven't seen them wheeled into the room. But now that we know what's going on, time is definitely of the essence."

Boris nods. "We should get out of here soon."

"I'm thinking tonight," Shadow continues. "I'm pretty sure one of the guards saw me and Noggin watching the procedure. It's only a matter of time before they come for us."

"So what's the game plan?" Jade asks.

"Noggin's family is ten floors below us," Shadow says. "If we can get down to them without being caught, maybe we can go back up the elevator and find a way to that ventilation shaft Jade was talking about."

Boris shakes his head. "There's no way we're making it back into the city through The Spire. Too many guards. We'll have to do this another way."

"And what's that?" demands Jade. "There's no other way out, is there?"

Boris pauses. "There is a rumor," he admits. "But it is only that. Nothing more."

"What's this rumor?" I ask with baited breath.

"There is a rumor that long ago, on the lowest level of the deepest, darkest dungeon, a secret escape tunnel was built. It's primary purpose was to aid The Dominion in getting supplies if The Spire ever came under siege. But no one who goes down to that level ever comes out alive. There's no way of knowing whether such a tunnel exists."

"Wait a second," I say. "Didn't they say they were moving my mother and sister down to the lowest level? If we can get to them, maybe we can find this tunnel!"

Shadow nods excitedly. "This could be our chance to get out! Where does this tunnel lead, Boris?"

"It is said that the secret tunnel leads out of the city, beyond the walls."

"That's perfect," Jade says. "What would we do without you, Boris?"

"It is only a rumor," Boris reminds us.

"But it's enough to go on," I say.

"And what if the tunnel doesn't exist?" Boris asks. "Then we'd be trapped fifteen stories below ground at the heart of The Dominion."

I shrug. "It's a chance we'll have to take if we want to get out of here. Who's with me?"

"I am," Shadow says, and Boris and Jade mumble their agreement as well.

"Alright," I say. "First things first- how are we going to get out of this cell?"

"How about with this?" Boris asks, and holds up a skinny metal key.

"Where'd you get that?" Jade exclaims.

"One of the guards dropped it while you guys were sleeping. I didn't want to wake you because I knew you'd make a lot of noise about it. Glad I waited."

"Let's get out of here!" I say, and Boris puts the key into the lock. He turns it, and with a metallic click, the lock pops open.

Chapter Twenty-One

The door slowly swings open. I keep expecting it to make a sound, but it doesn't. When it's finally open wide enough to get through, we exit the cell single-file, with Boris in the lead. The room is dark, with only a few torches lighting the stone walls.

We walk down the row of cages, back toward the door that leads out to the stone staircase. None of the prisoners make a sound- they're all either asleep, or too weak to say anything.

When we come to the thick wooden door, Boris pushes on it. Surprisingly, it's not locked.

"Seems odd," Shadow remarks.

I nod. "It's almost as if they wanted us to escape."

"Of course they don't," Jade whispers.

We quietly make our way out onto the stairs. The torches are still lighting the way, and it's eerily quiet as we climb further into the depths below The Spire. Water droplets make an otherworldly sound as they plummet from the low ceiling into small puddles on the stone steps.

"How far down do you think they are?" I whisper.

"The lowest level has to be pretty far down," Boris says. "I'm guessing at least another ten floors."

He's right, and when we finally come to the bottom of the stairs without running into anyone, I start to think that maybe we can get out of here. The staircase ends in a low stone hallway, leading to another wooden door. Boris goes up to it, and with a glance backward, turns the knob. It's not locked.

We walk through into a room similar to the upper levels of the dungeon, with cages on the walls. This room is much smaller, and most of the cages are empty. In fact, they all are, except for one on the other side of the room.

I run up to it. My mother and Flora are slumped against the wall, looking horribly emaciated and dirty. They aren't chained to anything, but they don't seem to be going anywhere.

My mother slowly crawls over to the edge of the cage and extends an arm through the bars. "What are you doing here, Noggin?" Her voice is weak and pained.

"I made a promise," I say, and I grab her hand.

Boris uses the key he picked up from the guard and unlocks the door. I walk into the cage and hug my mother and Flora for the first time in months. Boris, Shadow, and Jade all pile into the cell and join us.

"Let's get out of here," I say.

Suddenly, all the lights in the prison block go out except for one torch in the middle of the room. Three dark figures walk through the door, and the one in the middle speaks.

"What's going on here?" he demands, walking into the light, and with a sinking feeling, I realize our job just got a lot harder. Standing in the room, flanked by two Faceless, is Blackthorn.

Chapter Twenty-Two

He steps into the light of the torch, and for the first time not on a television screen, I am looking at Blackthorn. He's just as evil as he looks on screen. Greasy, jet black hair is slicked back from a pale forehead, above eyes as black as coal. He's wearing a jet black cloak that seems to be made from some type of expensive leather. At a gesture from Blackthorn, two of the guards lock the cell door again, leaving us in there with him and two Faceless.

He's not a very large man, but in the tiny, cramped space he commands a strange authority. I look over at Boris, Jade, and Shadow, huddled next to me up against the wall. On the other side of the cell, Flora and my mother are cowering in the corner, looking up at Blackthorn as he stares down at us with an unreadable expression. I make eye contact with Shadow, and I can tell he's just as scared as I am, and just as anxious to find out what is going to happen. Finally, Blackthorn speaks, in that calm, commanding voice.

"Why are you here?"

The room is absolutely silent. No one wants to speak.

"If no one wants to answer me, perhaps I should remind you that you are in my city, in my building," Blackthorn adds. He crouches down in front of Jade and puts a hand on her cheek. "Let's start with you. What's your name, my dear?"

I can tell that Jade is repulsed. She refuses to open her mouth. Blackthorn is not impressed.

"Alright," he says. "Let's all learn each other's names, shall we? He points at me. Your name, boy?"

"Ro-" I start to stutter, before Blackthorn interrupts me.

"Your real name."

I sigh. "My parents named me Noggin."

Blackthorn smiles menacingly as he claps slowly and theatrically. "That wasn't so hard, was it? And you?"

He points to Shadow, who reluctantly gives his name, followed by Boris and Jade. When he finally has all our names, he stands back up and faces away from us. The two Faceless that came into the cell with Blackthorn are whispering something to him. They've been watching us the whole time, or at least I think they have- it's impossible to tell with those masks. I hope that they don't recognize us. Boris and I exchange a nervous glance. After a minute, Blackthorn turns back to us.

"My guards tell me you four belong over in block nine," he says. "So what are you doing over here?"

"We got lost," Jade says.

Blackthorn chuckles. "You got lost all the way out of your locked and guarded cell?" He paces back and forth, shaking his head. "No, no no. I think you planned an escape, just like the way you must have planned your break in several weeks ago. The only thing missing was these two lovely ladies." He turns to Flora and my mother, who are still huddled in the corner, trying to avoid his eye. "You want them out of The Spire? Well, guess what? I can grant your wish… Noggin!" The last word is said with such contempt that it makes me even angrier.

He grabs my mother roughly by the shoulder. One of the Faceless opens the cell door, and Blackthorn drags my mother through and into the brighter light of the large torch in the center of the room. The Faceless follow, and find their place behind him. No one seems to be stopping us from coming out of the cell, so we do.

"What's he planning?" Jade whispers.

"Whatever it is, it can't be good," Shadow hisses back. I agree.

That's when Blackthorn pulls the knife from his robes and puts it to my mother's throat. She lets out a scream, but he tightens his grip. I feel Flora fall to her knees beside me, but I'm too busy staring at Blackthorn in horror to look over. Blackthorn starts to speak, loudly but calmly.

"Noggin, Shadow, Boris, and Jade. Don't waste your time trying to escape. You won't." He speaks calmly, while my mother's face holds a look of sheer terror.

"Instead, think of this: it is your fault you are imprisoned. You broke into my building, and for that you must be punished." He pauses, and tightens his hold on the knife. "Severely."

Next to me, Flora is whimpering, but I don't know what to do. We all stand there, frozen, as Blackthorn continues in his eerily calm voice.

"You think you know better than The Dominion. You think you can just walk in here and release my prisoners. You cannot."

His face turns from anger to pure rage, and as we look on in horror, Blackthorn slits my mother's throat and casts her to the ground.

Chapter Twenty-Three

The room is absolutely silent. No one moves or says anything. I can't believe what I've just seen. This can't be true- it just can't. After a few seconds of stunned silence, Flora starts screaming. She rushes toward Blackthorn, and I grab her, holding her back as she kicks and screams, fighting to get out of my grasp.

"You killed her!" she screams. "Why did you kill her?"

Blackthorn is still standing there, knife in hand. Behind him, the two Faceless stand silently, arms crossed. These must be his personal guards. I turn my gaze to the knife. My mother's blood is still dripping from the blade. I look down at her body, which lies in a quickly growing pool of crimson on the hard stone floor.

"How could you do this?" Jade snarls. "That woman had a family!"

Blackthorn hands the knife to one of his guards and slowly walks up to Jade, stopping only when his face is mere inches away from hers.

"So beautiful," he says calmly, his voice barely more than a whisper. "It's a shame you feel the need to associate yourself with such... scum." He gestures with a gloved hand to the rest of us.

"Go to hell," Jade snarls, and spits in his face. Blackthorn's guards immediately step forward, but they stop when he calmly raises a hand.

"You're wrong, my dear," he says, wiping the spit off his face with his glove. "She doesn't have a family. None of you do. No one cares about you. You can pretend that people love you, that people care about you- but at the end of the day, everyone is alone in this world. You are born alone, and you will die alone."

"You're wrong." I speak up, finally finding my tongue. "She did have a family. I was her son. And I promised my father that I would get her out of here. You messed with the wrong family, Blackthorn." From the corner of my eye, I can see Boris moving slowly toward the guards. I realize that he's planning something, and whatever it is, I have to keep Blackthorn talking, and distracted.

"You're the one with no family," I continue. "You rule over us, and you torture us. You're a murderer. You treat us like scum, but you're the real scum here, Blackthorn."

Blackthorn turns to me, and looks me over silently.

He steps forward, and I can feel his rancid breath on my face.

"You said you were her son," he breathes, and something changes in his expression. "You can say whatever you want. You're never leaving this prison, Thornslayer!"

That's when Boris lunges forward and grabs a grenade from one of the guards' belts. "Like hell," he says, and pulls the pin.

Shadow jumps forward and punches the other guard in the face as the explosion shakes the room, before grabbing another grenade off the guard's belt and pulling the pin. This one is apparently a smoke grenade, because the chamber starts to fill with smoke.

It's not a very big room, so after about thirty seconds it's impossible to see anything. I close my eyes to avoid being blinded by the smoke. I feel someone grab my sleeve and start dragging me away from the guards. I can hear Blackthorn shouting at the Faceless to get back up. I hear a door open- it must be the trapdoor that Boris found-

and then I open my eyes to find myself at the bottom of a short ladder, in a tunnel. Boris is already in there with me. Shadow, Jade, and Flora quickly jump through the door after us. Boris climbs up and slams the door shut behind us, leaving us in pitch darkness.

PART III
THE ESCAPE

Chapter Twenty-Four

We take off down the tunnel with Boris in the lead. He's followed closely by Jade, Flora, and myself, with Shadow bringing up the rear. I'm running forward as fast as I can, but it's pitch dark and all I can think of is my mother. My poor mother. She had never done anything remotely against the law, at least to my knowledge. For Blackthorn to kill her so quickly and easily without a second thought; that was the mark of true evil. Both of my parents have now been killed by The Dominion. I can only imagine what Flora must be thinking right now- she's so young. It's not right that both her parents should be dead. They're my parents too, and I'm on the verge of vomiting and passing out at the same time. It must be so much worse for her.

Up ahead, Boris has found a torch on the wall and lit it. In the gloom, all our faces look gaunt and ill. Flora sits down on the floor against the wall and begins to cry. It takes everything I have not to join her, but I must stay strong.

"Come on, Flora," I say. "We've got to keep moving."

She sniffles and looks up at me. "To where?"

"Away from here," I reply in a choked voice, and help her up.

We keep moving. After about an hour, Boris comes to a halt.

"We'll rest here," he says.

"Is it safe?" asks Shadow. "They could be right on our tail!"

Boris turns to Shadow angrily. "Do you hear them coming?"

Shadow shakes his head. It's absolutely silent.

"Then we'll rest," Boris says through his teeth. "We can't have anyone collapsing from exhaustion."

He's right. The only thing keeping me going at this point is the thought of getting Flora away from here. The Cell has never been a safe place by any means, but now that Blackthorn knows about us it's even more dangerous.

After we've rested for a few minutes, Boris finally

stands up. He has managed to grab a vest from one of the guards, which has several grenades and three swords. He gives one of the swords to me and one to Shadow.

"Let's hope we don't need these," he simply says, and starts back down the tunnel. The rest of us follow his lead, even though we're so tired we can barely stand. With heavy feet and heavier hearts, we continue on down the tunnel, toward whatever unknown destination lies at the end.

Chapter Twenty-Five

I'm not exactly sure how much time has passed. It feels like we've been walking for a very long time, but it could be anywhere from ten minutes to ten hours. The tunnel hasn't sloped up or down at all, but we must be nearing the edge of the city by now. Nobody says much for quite some time, but after a while Shadow speaks up.

"What are we going to do when we get out?"

I haven't really thought about it. My main goal, of course, is getting Flora to safety.

"We don't even know if there will be anything at the end of this tunnel," Jade says. "It could very well be a dead end."

Boris shakes his head. "This has to be the tunnel from the legend, leading out of the city. There's no way it'd be this long otherwise. The only thing I'm worried about is the ceiling being collapsed somewhere up ahead."

I hadn't thought of that. If the tunnel was blocked anywhere along the way, we would surely be captured and killed. Once Blackthorn and The Faceless figured out where we'd gone, they'd be hot on our heels with enough men to ensure we didn't get away this time.

"What are we going to do about food?" I ask. "I haven't eaten for days, and I'm sure Flora wasn't exactly well fed either."

She nods. "We were lucky. They fed us, but I don't know why."

I know why. It's because they wanted to keep my mother and Flora alive to torture them for information. Tears sting my eyes as I remember the look on my mother's face while Blackthorn slit her throat. But I have to be strong for Flora. I wipe my eyes and keep walking.

The hours drag on, with no change in the slope of the tunnel. I start to wonder if we'll ever get out of here. I can hardly see, and the torch Boris carries is running very low on flame.

A few hours later, the torch finally goes out and we are left in absolute darkness. I've never experienced such an overwhelming feeling of hopelessness and claustrophobia. We stand there silently in the darkness for several minutes. I can hear Boris scraping rocks together, trying to get the flame started again. Finally, he stops.

"It's not working."

Flora lets out a sob. I put my arm around her and tell her it'll be alright. We continue walking, carefully in the absolute darkness.

After a while, I hear Boris hissing at us to stop and be quiet from up ahead. In the darkness, hearing takes over as the most powerful sense. I can't seem to hear anyone behind us, which is good. From ahead, however, is the sound of-

"Water!" Flora exclaims. "I can hear water!"

"There are stairs here!" Boris shouts. We climb the stairs. When we get to the top after about forty steps, we're all crowded in a small enclosed area.

"There's a ladder here!" Shadow says. "Boris, you go first."

Boris climbs the ladder, and after a minute his voice drifts down from far above. "There's a trapdoor! I'm opening it!"

We all wait with baited breath as Boris struggles with the door. As he finally gets it open, a sliver of light drifts down. We all cheer. It's a small victory, but this is getting us one step closer to freedom, and one step further away from The Cell. Jade and Flora start climbing up the ladder. I start to follow them, but Shadow grabs my arm.

"So, are we going to talk about what happened back there?"

"What?" I say. "How they killed my mother in front of my little sister?"

"Blackthorn called you Thornslayer."

"Oh. I know, why do you think he did that?" I'm genuinely confused by Shadow's interest in this.

Shadow continues. "Several years ago, when my sister escaped from the city, she was helped by a man by the name of Thornslayer. The Thornslayer family is known all over the city as the leader of the secret rebellion against The Dominion."

I'm shocked. "Do you think my father was part of this family?"

Shadow shrugs. "You'd know better than I. Can you remember anything about what your father did? Anything at all?"

I shake my head. "I had nothing to do with any of it."

"Don't you see what you've done?" He sighs. "It doesn't matter if you're actually involved in the rebellion or not. We broke into The Spire, and Blackthorn called you Thornslayer. The Thornslayer family have always been a direct threat to The Dominion. That's why he killed your father."

"What does this all mean?" I ask.

Shadow slams his fist into the wall angrily. "This means he will hunt you down, as well as your family and friends. And he will never stop until you are dead."

I'm almost at a loss for words. "If Blackthorn thinks I'm a threat to The Dominion, that means Flora is in grave danger."

"We all are," Shadow replies gravely. "The best thing to do right now is to get as far away from the city as possible."

I nod. Getting Flora to safety is the main goal now.

Chapter Twenty-Six

I climb halfway up the ladder, then pause and look up at the sky. It's still overcast, but after the darkness of the tunnel the outdoors seem much brighter. Shadow and I climb the rest of the way up and we all stand there, looking around in shock.

The trapdoor has opened onto a narrow strip of

rocky beach. Behind us is the outside of the massive wall of The Cell, stretching up out of sight into the smoky clouds. In front of us is dark, choppy water, as far as the eye can see. There's nowhere to go except left or right, where we will surely be caught. Thinking quickly, I turn to Boris.

"Let's block the trapdoor to buy us some time."

Boris agrees, and we spread out to search for something heavy enough to hold it down. After a while, Flora cries out from down the beach.

"I think this'll work, but I can't lift it on my own!"

We all run over to her, where she stands next to a rock measuring about three feet across.

"We could put this right over the trapdoor!" She says excitedly. Jade tries pushing the rock- it doesn't budge. With great effort, Boris, Shadow, and I manage to pick it up together and carry it over to the trap door. With a satisfying thud, it hits the ground.

"That should hold it," says Boris, wiping the dirt from his hands on his pants. "Nobody's coming through there without a battering ram." He mops his brow.

"Where should we go now?" I ask. "There's no point sticking around here, especially with the Faceless on our tail."

Jade nods in agreement. "Let's walk along the wall. There has to be a road or something that leads to the front gates."

"It's a good idea in theory," Shadow says, "but if we head for the main gate, we're basically walking back into the arms of The Dominion."

He's got a point, but I don't see any other option.

"How about this," Boris interjects. "We'll walk along the wall and look for some sort of road or bridge leading out of here. If we see anyone coming- anyone at all- we'll hide underwater."

"Then what?" Jade asks. "I don't know about you guys, but I can't swim well at all."

None of us can, but for now it's the best plan we've got. If we stay here we're sitting ducks, so we start making our way down the beach. All our belongings were left back in the dungeon, so we travel light- all we have are the swords and grenades that Boris managed to steal.

For about a half hour, we walk slowly along. Boris walks slightly ahead of the rest, closely followed by Shadow. Jade walks alone in the middle, and Flora and I bring up the rear.

As we walk, there is no change in scenery- just the wall of the city to our left, the rocky beach below our feet, the seemingly endless ocean to our right, and the usual misty smoke in the air. Just when it seems as if we'll never find our way to safety, Boris shouts out from ahead.

"I can see something! There's a pile of rocks up ahead!"

We all look up and see what he's referring to. The rocks block our view of what's ahead- it's the perfect place to rest and decide what to do next. We make our way up to the rocks. While the others sit down, hidden from view, Shadow and I climb up to the top. When we can finally see past the blockade, my jaw drops.

We are standing at the top of a massive slope. At

the bottom, on the left stand the main gates of the city, closed and locked. A bridge, not more than ten feet wide, stretches to the right from the gates off into the ocean, where it disappears into the mist.

"Wow," Shadow breathes from next to me. "I wonder where that bridge leads?"

"I don't know," I reply. "Maybe we should go scout it out. You know, before we all stumble down there."

Shadow nods in agreement, and we climb back down to the others. Boris is putting his coat around Flora, who is shivering from the cold breeze blown in from sea. I nod my thanks to him. She's my sister, I should be protecting her.

"Boris, you're going to want to take a look at this," Shadow says.

Boris gets up, leaving his jacket with Flora and Jade.

"Stay here," he says. "We're just going up there for a minute."

Boris, Shadow and I walk up to the top of the hill

again. Boris draws a breath.

"Wow."

"Do you think there's a way to get to the bridge without being seen?" I ask.

"Hard to tell from here," Boris replies. "Why don't you and Shadow go check it out?"

Shadow and I look at each other. I can still remember meeting him for the first time, only weeks before. We've been through so much together since then, I feel like I've known him my entire life.

"We can do that," I say. Shadow nods, and we start climbing down the slope.

It's steep and rocky, so the going is slow. After about 30 minutes, I stop and look back up. We're barely halfway down, and if the gates open now we're in plain sight. We press on.

The air isn't hot, but Shadow and I are both dripping in sweat by the time we reach the bottom of the hill. To our left are the massive gates of the city, cold and unforgiving. To the right is a small set of stairs leading directly up to the bridge.

    We climb the stairs and emerge onto the bridge. I look back up the hill, where I can just barely see Boris standing on the rocks. I raise my arm and beckon to him.

    "Do you think he can see us?" I ask Shadow.

    "I sure hope so. I don't want to make that climb again," he replies. I can't help but agree.

    It appears Boris has seen us, for after briefly disappearing back behind the rocks he reappears with Flora and Jade and they start climbing down. For the next hour, Shadow and I sit restlessly, expecting the doors to come crashing open any minute. But they don't.

    When Boris, Jade, and Flora finally make it to the bridge, there's no time to rest. We set off at a fast pace away from the city. I start to believe that maybe, just maybe, we've made it away safely. I can get Flora to a safe place where she can grow up. Maybe she won't have a normal childhood, but at least she won't have to grow up in The Cell. But that all depends on what lies at the other end of this bridge. Is it another city? I can only imagine, but hopefully we can find help there.

    I'm jarred from my thoughts by the all-too-familiar sound of the curfew alarm. We must be at least a mile away from the city, but it's still incredibly loud. The alarm stops after a minute. We come to a halt, wondering what's going on. It's only about 2 pm. Boris and I exchange a nervous glance.

    A loud creaking noise comes from the city. In an instant, I realize what's going on, and I now know that we're in bigger trouble than we thought. The doors of The Cell are opening. I've never seen this happen before. Even from this far away, the gate looks huge. The creaking sound stops as the doors come to a halt. It's absolutely silent for a minute, and then the air is filled with the sound of a multitude of footsteps as several hundred Faceless pour out of the city toward us.

Chapter Twenty-Seven

    For a few crucial seconds that seem to contain an eternity, we keep still and look at the advancing army in shock. I turn and look away from the city at the bridge, stretching farther than the eye can see. Running doesn't seem to be an option.

"We're gonna have to fight," I say, and draw my sword. From the corner of my eye, I see Shadow and Boris do the same. Flora is hanging back- she's never been a fighter. I realize that she'll be the first to die when all hell breaks loose.

I go over to the edge of the bridge and look over. At this point, I estimate the water is about one hundred feet below us- way too far to jump. Boris comes over and looks down at the supports.

"Hold on," he says, climbing up onto the railing. We all draw a breath.

"What are you doing?" Jade cries.

"Sometimes on a bridge like this, there'll be a storage space underneath," Boris explains. "Flora could probably fit in there and be safe from the fight." He points at a small enclosed space under the bridge. "See? There it is!"

I turn and look at Flora, who is visibly shaking. "Come on!"

We all help her climb over the railing, and Boris doesn't let go until she is safely underneath. She crawls in so far that we can't see her, and the reappears almost instantly.

"Guys- there's a boat under here!" She crawls out of the hole to the point where half of her body is hanging out over the edge. "It has oars and everything!"

We all look at each other in astonishment.

"Could we use it to escape?" Jade exclaims.

"We might be able to," Boris replies. "It'd be a long drop though. We'd have to-"

His response is cut short by the sound of the approaching Faceless, now less than two hundred feet away. There are hundreds of them, and only three of us. There's no way we're fighting our way out of this. Shadow is under the bridge with Flora, frantically trying to get the boat out. Boris turns to Jade, grabbing her shoulder.

"Listen closely, because there's no time for me to

say this twice."

She nods.

"I need you to get in there and help get the boat. It's our only chance of getting out of here alive. If we all get in, we might be able to hold the boat steady enough to get it in the water, hopefully with minimal injury. Noggin and I will do our best to hold them off." He glances at me, and our eyes meet. I'm sure we both realize that the chances of us making it out are slim. But that doesn't mean we can't try. I steel myself and turn back to the bridge.

In an instant, the Faceless are on us like hornets. The first row draw their swords and attack. I parry the first blow with my sword, but the second one nicks my arm. I feel the hot blood run down my sleeve, and I launch into a counterattack with everything I've got.

Next to me, Boris is fighting off three or four Faceless with ease. He's taller than most of them, so it's not really a fair fight. Thankfully, the bridge isn't wide enough to allow very many through at once.

I glance over and see Shadow, Flora and Jade

pulling the boat out from underneath the bridge. It's sticking about halfway out, and I realize that it's now or never.

"Come on, Boris!" I shout, and leap over the edge, landing next to Jade. She grabs my arm and steadies the boat, which is balanced precariously on the ledge. We all look up and see Boris being overrun with Faceless.

"Drop it! Drop it now!" he shouts, and wrenches a grenade from his vest. He pulls the pin, tosses the grenade, and the Faceless scatter. Boris runs through them and leaps over the railing as the bridge erupts in fire, sending the boat flying through the air. We fall for what seems like an eternity, and when we finally hit the water it feels like landing on rock.

I emerge from the water with a gasp. The boat is sitting about twenty feet away, miraculously upright. There's no sign of the others. I make my way over to the boat and climb in. Shadow's head bobs up into view from over by the bridge. Soon after, Jade and Flora emerge from the water and climb into the boat. They are soaking wet, but don't seem to be harmed. Shadow swims over from the bridge, which has a huge chunk blown out of it. There's a lot of rubble everywhere, and smoke has filled the air.

As Shadow makes his way into the boat with Jade's help, I turn my gaze to the wreckage. Several minutes pass, and there's still no sign of Boris anywhere. The waves eventually become calm again, but the floating wreckage remains still.

I turn to Shadow, and I'm sure he knows what we're all thinking. He meets my eyes and slightly shakes his head. The boat slowly rocks on the waves, and we all sit there silently.

Chapter Twenty-Eight

The silence is broken by Shadow seemingly coming to his senses and grabbing two oars from the bottom of the boat.

"Come on, now," he says. "We won't get away by just sitting here."

Wordlessly, I take one of the oars. As we start to

paddle away from the wreckage, the reality of what just happened starts to sink in.

"Shouldn't we go back and look for Boris?" Flora asks, her voice quivering. "After all, he was the one who really got us out of there."

None of us can disagree with that, but Shadow says what I'm sure most of us are thinking:

"It'd be suicide. You saw how many Faceless were back there. You think they all went back to The Spire and forgot about us?" He mops his brow and continues paddling. "Besides, we made it this far. Do you really think he'd want us to go back now?"

No one says anything. As the boat makes its way through the water, the smoke starts to clear, only to be replaced by a heavy mist.

"This is good," Shadow says, clearly trying to cheer us all up. "If we can't see them, they can't see us."

"We can never see them," Jade replies. "They wear masks- that's the point."

No one laughs. Her attempt at humor is a nice

gesture, but it does little to lighten the mood.

I turn my attention to the contents of the boat. There's not much- the two oars, five gallons of water, a fishing rod, and several small packages with the word "RAMEN" printed on them- evidently some type of food rations. We'll have to save them. This is uncharted territory, and no one knows how long we'll have to stay in this boat. I estimate about a week or so before one of us resorts to cannibalism. I put my oar down and take a seat, staring into the mist as Shadow continues paddling.

Flora comes over and sits by my side, and I put my arm around her. In a world where so many things are evil and crazy, it feels good to be able to comfort the only person left in this world that I love.

"Do you think they'll come looking for us?" she asks.

"The Faceless?" I reply, brushing the hair out of her face.

"Yeah."

I look down at her.

"Probably," I reply. "But if they do, we'll put up one hell of a fight."

That's the last thing any of us say for a while. I watch as the fog creeps in, slowly obscuring the city from view. Soon it's just us and the open ocean. Shadow continues to paddle, carrying us farther and farther away from the city we've all called home for our whole lives. Jade finally breaks the silence.

"I don't know if I could ever really force myself to go back there," she says sadly. "Even if there's nothing else out here." She twists a lock of her bright green hair.

The others nod in agreement, especially Flora, but I keep still and continue staring into the distance. I have to go back. There's no other option. I'd been hoping that once I got Flora out, I'd be able to turn away from this place and the evil within it. But I now know that is impossible. I am a member of the Thornslayer family.

I close my eyes for a moment, and all I can see is my mother's face as Blackthorn slit her throat. Murdered in cold blood for a crime committed by no one.

I open my eyes and take one last look through the mist, back toward the city I grew up in. Despite all this, despite everything we have lost, I know that I am not done with the place. I will return one day; and when I do, it will be to kill Blackthorn. With that thought, I turn my gaze away from everything I've ever known, and stare into the great unknown that lies before us.

TO BE CONTINUED

Acknowledgements:

There are many people without whom The Blackthorn Chronicles would not have been possible. My sincerest thanks to:

Rory Washburn, my good friend and editor. Without your constant reading and rereading of the manuscript, I'd still be on Chapter One.

My parents, for their unwavering support and encouragement, but most importantly for instilling in me at a very young age the importance of reading.

And finally, anyone who is reading this. Thank you! It means the world to me and I hope you enjoy the story of Noggin Thornslayer.

ABOUT THE AUTHOR

Benjamin Holmquist was born in New England, where he was homeschooled before attending the University of Southern Maine.

The Blackthorn Chronicles is his first novel.

PORTLAND PUBLIC LIBRARY SYSTEM
5 MONUMENT SQUARE
PORTLAND, ME 04101

WITHDRAWN